BLOOD KISSED

CHOSEN VAMPIRE SLAYER

MILA YOUNG

JORDAN CROW

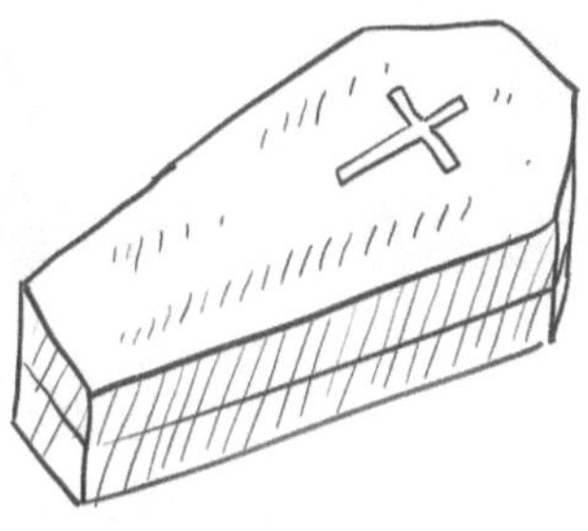

"He isn't giving you a choice anymore," I said. "Either you let him go, or you go with him." I could feel Veronica watching me closely.

"I can't," she murmured. "I can't go with him."

"I know," I said. "Because we would never let you. We would follow you to the ends of the earth, to the furthest corners of time and space. There is nothing that could spare him from our wrath."

Veronica snuggled into my chest. I sensed her smile, although her face was hidden. "I'm not afraid of you, Orion," she said softly.

I forced the beast to stay dormant. The fangs in my mouth barely managed not to burst forth. I did not succumb to the raging tide of bloodlust.

"You don't need to fear me," I said to Veronica. "I don't want you to."

CONTENTS

CHOSEN VAMPIRE SLAYER

Night Kissed
Moon Kissed
Blood Kissed

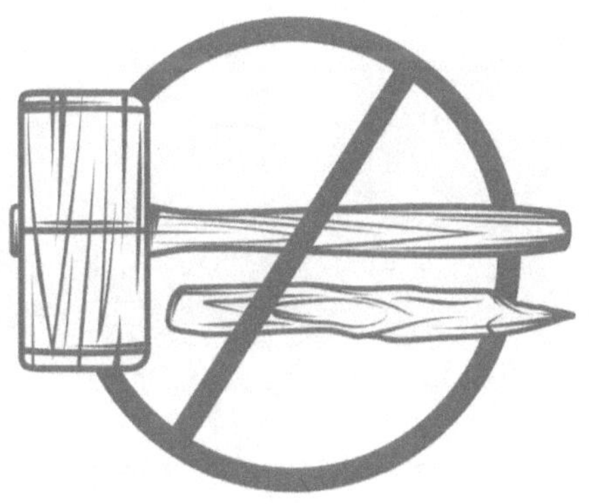

BLOOD KISSED

Torn by loyalty and the fiery desires of a conflicted heart, Veronica finds herself at a crossroads. What will she do if burning love turns into cold regret?

This is your kind of book if you love kick-ass heroines with sass to match, scorching hot monsters who take what they want, and is perfect for devourers of enemies to lovers books. Expect steam, action, and a supernatural world filled with vampires, demons, shifters, angels... and unhinged alphas who will do anything to protect their woman. Lovers of Anita Blake and True Blood, this is your next addiction.

PROLOGUE

VERONICA

I had no idea how fast we were moving. All I knew was that if I looked down, the ground whipped by at a truly unsettling speed. And if I somehow managed to turn around, I was willing to bet Lian's house would be long gone, lost in the distance.

Okay, Veronica. Take a deep breath. You can figure this out.

I tried to follow my own advice and quickly discovered a deep breath was out of the question because of the way my ribs were being crushed in the vise grip of bony fingers. That left only step two to worry about: Figure this out before panic swallowed me.

Instead, I thrashed against the monster holding onto me, kicking and punching, which did nothing but make him move faster. His grip was iron, and I wasn't getting out of his hold easily.

"Oh yeah," I muttered under my breath. "No problem." Again, I glanced at the ground. We were far beyond the manicured lawns of Lian's neighborhood. Now there was black dirt and patches of snow. Rugged tree trunks flashed by, dangerously close to the top of my skull. I didn't want to lose my head.

The view in the other direction wasn't great either. I twisted my head around, shaking the loose hair out of my face. The dark silhouette of the wendigo loomed above me, glowing eyes fixed forward, exposed bones shining dully under a ragged pelt of skin and fur. Of all the shitty situations I'd gotten myself into over the years, this one definitely ranked among the ugliest.

Focus, V. The little voice in my head grew stern. *By the looks of this thing, once you get wherever the hell you're going, you won't have much time.* Staring up at the beast, I had to agree. But my current predicament was complicated. As far as I knew, there was nothing stopping the wendigo from crushing me to death at the slightest hint of insubordination. It sure didn't seem like I was destined to serve any higher purpose other than food.

Maybe I could get it to drop me…but did I

really want that? The wind whipped my hair so hard I thought it might pull out at the roots. A fall from this height from the edge of the hill, at this speed, could easily kill me; if not now, a few agonizing minutes or hours later. Assuming I didn't die on impact, would I be able to get to safety?

So, yeah, it actually felt kind of strange to know I was on my own, at least for now. There was no doubt in my mind that the second Orion got wind of the current unfolding disaster, he'd be coming for me. And I'd be glad to see him.

But I had no way of predicting when that would be, or how long it would take him to track me down. For now, it was me, myself, and I against a feral undead monstrosity.

I tried to brace myself against the top of its hand without drawing any attention, but the moment I started wriggling to get out of its grip again, I felt those long fingers tighten. All the air rushed out of my lungs as if they were deflating balloons. My initial instincts were right on the money: It would just keep squeezing until I was dead.

"Shit," I gasped. My face was flushed with the effort each breath demanded. I could barely feel the blood rushing into my cheeks, they'd gone so numb from the cold. Wild as it was, I knew this part of Alaska like the back of my hand, and my gut told me we'd changed course. That probably wasn't good.

"God damn it, I need to get out of here." I sucked up as much oxygen as I could force into my lungs and pushed with all my might, until every muscle in my body screamed. My legs kicked out and connected with something hard. A searing pain shot through my foot. I squeezed my eyes shut. "Bad idea. Bad idea."

Suddenly, my perspective changed. The cold air sliced like a razor blade across my face, stinging my eyes with tears. I grimaced but kept up the struggle. The world spun wildly, end over end, and I realized that I was swinging as the wendigo made another turn. Another tree trunk whipped by, and almost as an afterthought, I reached out for whatever I might be able to grab.

Could I have broken my hands in a million places and screwed myself over completely? Yes. Fortunately, luck was at least a little on my side. I caught on to a branch, and the momentum of the wendigo's movement helped it tear free. Although it wasn't very clear how big my new weapon was in the shadowy darkness, it felt nice and heavy. And it was probably sharp on the end. Unbalanced, but as a present beggar, I couldn't afford to be a chooser.

I adjusted my grip on the broken branch. The right angle was hard to determine in the first place, let alone land. My hair flew all over the place, and I had this crazy, surreal thought that it was gonna take forever to get all the tangles out. As if I wasn't being slung around like a ragdoll by some otherworldly beast who'd just kidnapped me out of my bed.

"Hey!" The howling wind stole my voice right off my lips, and at first I thought the wendigo hadn't heard me at all. Then a shift in its rickety armature of bone and sinew sent shudders through the ghastly body, and I saw it turn its head to look at me. The eyes, glowing with a furious but empty fire, bored into me.

This was it; now or never. I clenched my teeth and took the only shot I knew I was ever going to have.

All I remember of the moments following the strike was the shrill, pain-driven screech tearing over the treetops. The wendigo recoiled from the branch now protruding from one of its eyes, and I had to squeeze mine shut in order to handle the g-forces put upon me by its frantic flailing. My ears rang. I fought to keep my head and neck steady.

Yet with every swing of the creature's gangly arms, I felt everything grow dimmer and more distant.

It was like being drowned in violent, freezing water. My heart pounded in my chest. I struggled to breathe.

I hope it hurts, you bastard, I thought viciously through the pain. *I hope it hurts real fucking bad.*

But if I had hoped to get the wendigo to stop, or even slow it down, I was sorely disappointed. The ground continued to race by, although not as smoothly. The wendigo's movements had become erratic and unpredictable, perhaps owing to its new, half-blind condition. Occasionally it stumbled, and I'd be thrown haphazardly into the air as it attempted to regain balance. The lunging motion turned my stomach, but at least at the height of each dizzying swing, I could see far into the distance. This was the point at which I learned instead of heading back to the lair in Chugach State Park, we were traveling straight north.

"I knew it," I whispered. My lungs burned. The vague sense of triumph only lasted until my next glimpse ahead, which was when I realized exactly where we were going. In fact, its massive peak soared high above the horizon, gleaming white even in the dead of the Alaskan night. As correct as my instincts had been, the reality of our destination caught me off guard.

Why would a thing like this take me to Denali? The mountain embodied everything sacred about Alaska's wild frontier. It was steeped in ancient magic, mystical traditions older than memory, older than time. I was quite sure, even in my limited knowledge, that there was no place for a monster there.

I had to stop it.

"Hey!" I yelled again, squirming in the wendigo's grasp. "You want another branch to the face, buddy? 'Cause I can hook you up!" This time, instead of tightening, the wendigo's grip weakened for just a second. It was enough time for me to yank all but one leg free. I perched on the edge of its huge, bony hand, waiting for my next window of opportunity. "Trip again," I muttered under my breath. "I dare you. It'll be the last fucking time."

While I waited, my whole body tense as live wires, I scanned the surrounding environment for another improvised weapon. Ironically, the grievous wound I had inflicted on the wendigo worked against me, especially since I no longer had the anchor of its hand keeping me in place. One wrong move and I'd be splattered.

I frowned. Maybe that was better than the

alternative. If I had to go out, I wanted to be able to choose my own terms. *Whoa there, V. Survival is still the best-case scenario. Don't go full fatalist just yet.* Although my eyes were trained on what I could see of the wendigo's ugly mug, my mind's eye wandered to the three faces I had come to admire so intensely.

Logan. Seth. And, of course, Orion. What would they do if I was killed tonight? How would they feel? Would they swear revenge, like I had after losing Dylan? Part of me kind of liked to think so. But an even bigger part didn't want to find out.

"Nope, no dying for Veronica today."

The wendigo pitched unsteadily forward. I braced myself.

"Sorry, man. I've got other things to do." Three other things, specifically. I decided right then and there that I couldn't die happy until I'd done each of them at least one more time. And that meant death was off the table.

The wendigo's loping stride faltered severely. I felt myself thrown forward into freefall as its hand opened, fingers fanning out. It looked like the chance I had waited for so patiently, and I got ready to seize it for all it was worth.

But then it all came crashing down. Instead of

tucking and rolling onto the half-frozen, unyielding ground, I ended up dangling upside down, my calf pinched precariously between the tips of two claws. The luck that had come through so quick for me minutes earlier had just unceremoniously run out. Once my head stopped spinning, I rolled my eyes up and stared directly into the monster's baleful, one-eyed gaze. The tree branch still stuck brutally out from one socket.

"Let go," I growled, "or I'll do it again."

It lifted me slowly, inspecting me from all angles. I couldn't have looked like much of a prize, all disheveled, my hair in knots. For a moment, I thought it might toss its head back and drop me straight into its dark, skeletal maw. Then the claws opened, releasing my leg. I dropped roughly into the grasp of its other hand. My neck whipped painfully backward on impact.

"Fuck," I hissed. Stars exploded behind my eyes. "Not good." When I dared to look again, I saw the wendigo staring at me with its single good eye. And I felt its grip closing down on my torso, compressing my chest. The air came first in short bursts, then in ragged gasps, then not at all.

That blazing, hollow eye was the last thing in my view before it all went black.

CHAPTER 1

SETH

Logan was waiting for me outside of the Rabbit's Foot bar, half in shadow, quietly watching the world go by. I hadn't seen him in the flesh since the start of my little vacation in the Underworld. He looked at me as I approached, just a casual flick of the eyes.

"Hey," I said. "Been a minute." The way his cold blue eyes glowed in the darkness reminded me of some things I had seen on the other side of the veil. Kind of made me wonder how different angels and demons really were.

"Yeah." He straightened up. "Good to see you."

I smirked. "You're just saying that."

Logan chuckled. "You think I want to do all this shit by myself? Hell no." He stepped away from the bar and started down the street, his gaze picking over every face that passed us by. I followed suit, but in the washed-out light of the bars and street-lights, it was hard to tell a normal human from a vamp. They all looked sallow, sunken-eyed, and mostly miserable to me.

"I bet we won't find a single one of these idiots," I muttered. We were supposed to be searching for survivors of the clan massacre that I had witnessed through the mirror, which seemed ironic. Not because Orion had asked us to do it—wouldn't any shepherd want to track down his scattered flock? There was just something funny about a legion of dead-ass vamps "surviving" anything. What did survival mean to someone who slept in a coffin every night?

"We'd better." Logan's face was impassive, but I could hear the edge of irritation in his voice. "I was tracking something when he called me back to the house."

I gave him a sidelong glance. "What do you mean by 'something'? You mean the thing that almost beat him and his whole cult to death?"

The angel nodded. "Yes. The thing you used as a gateway to get back here. It's a wendigo, by the way."

I almost stopped walking. "Man, fuck, Orion. If

you had a bead on it, you should've just ignored him and kept on Wendigo's trail."

"That's not what I agreed to," he said calmly.

My temper flared, and I opened my mouth to continue berating him. I wanted to say he was weak, that he was a follower, that I hoped he enjoyed his life as a sycophant, because it was all he'd ever be. *Who fucking gives a shit about agreements anymore?* In my eyes, the loss of his clan had all but stripped Orion of the power he'd leveraged to rope us into his schemes.

Then again, there we were. Both of us—Logan and me. I told myself I wasn't doing anything for Orion anymore, only Veronica. But that still meant beating the pavement in the dead of night, hunting down what was left of his followers.

I closed my mouth and took a deep breath, willing the anger in my veins to cool. "Listen, I appreciate you helping me out like that. Thank you."

Logan glanced my way. "You could have stayed there," he said, smiling slightly. "Never would've seen Orion again."

"And he never would've missed me." I grinned. "Trust me, I thought about it. But somehow, slowly freezing to death in a barren wasteland seemed like the worse—"

That was when I felt it—a shockwave rippling through the realm. It hit me like an electric shock, mild but jarring enough to instantly grab my attention. I paused mid-stride and stared off into the distance. There was nothing to see except a cold, murky night, but I knew somewhere, something had gone wrong.

"You too?" Logan's voice sounded like it came from miles away. He stood beside me with the same expression of puzzled concern.

"Yeah." I ran my fingers through my hair. "I don't—"

Then suddenly, a bolt of understanding came down from out of the blue. In my mind, I could see the threads connecting us to Veronica straining under the pull of an unexpectedly violent force. The details were murky, but one thing was absolutely certain.

She was in trouble.

Just as I was thinking it, Logan spoke my thoughts aloud. "It's V," he said. "There's something wrong with her."

We had yet to locate a single wayward member of Orion's clan, but my priorities had abruptly shifted. I no longer gave a rat's ass about the clan— and this time I had a feeling the vamp might actually agree with me.

"I have to go," I told Logan. "Right now. Wherever she is, I need to find her." Without waiting for an answer, I spun around and headed in the direction my senses told me. I figured Logan would fire straight back to Orion and let him know I'd defected from our stupid assignment. But when I glanced to my left, he was rushing alongside me instead.

"You're not going alone," he stated flatly by way of an explanation. "I have a feeling you're going to need help."

"Thanks for the vote of confidence," I replied. Still, as much as it pained me to admit, I felt some measure of relief in the knowledge that I had backup. There was no telling what we were getting ourselves into.

"You're welcome," Logan said without a trace of irony. He paused briefly before continuing. "Actually, don't thank me yet. We have to tell Orion."

And there it was. The temper I'd wrangled into submission a few minutes ago threatened to rear its ugly head again. The absolute last thing I wanted to do was get the vamp involved. I could work with Logan. I could even peacefully coexist with him, despite the common assumptions about angels and demons. But all of my lenience toward

Orion had been consumed by having to save his life.

"Do we?" I asked. My tone of voice made it clear as day that this was a plan I did not support. "All he's gonna do is take credit while we do most of the work."

Logan frowned. "Sounds like you think it'd be a good idea to hide information about Veronica from him until he inevitably finds out and shit hits the fan. Orion isn't as stupid or oblivious as you like to think, Seth. He's just as connected to her as we are."

"He was mortal, though," I pointed out. As far as I was concerned, Orion's human roots were a significant weakness. No amount of strength, speed, or immortality would ever fully erase the inferior being he had been in the past.

Logan, however, was unfazed. "And now he's not," he said simply. "Get over it." At the next inter-section, he veered in the general direction of Orion's house. "I'm willing to work with you, Seth. The only thing I care about right now is Veronica's well-being, and if we're on the same page, great. But Orion needs to know what's happening as soon as possible. This is one of the few circum-stances where I believe he might actually set aside differences and help."

I still didn't like it, and I grumbled under my breath even as I redirected my course to follow his. "Tell me it doesn't grind your goddamn gears to share her. I fucking dare you."

Logan shrugged. The moon broke through a cover of deep purple clouds, reflecting silver off his hair and skin. "As a demon, you ought to know it isn't that unusual."

I thought back to ages I had spent in fiery circles of Hell, surrounded by countless naked bodies in various states of ecstasy. The point he had made was one I had trouble disputing. "Fine," I said. "But with Orion specifically? I can barely handle sharing a house with him. Or space. Or, you know, air."

Logan didn't answer right away. "It's not my ideal," he admitted at last. "Mostly because I think Orion would claim her for himself if given half a chance." A flicker of some restrained emotion moved across his face. Was it annoyance? Disgust? Disdain?

I shook my head. "Someday, I'm gonna see you get pissed. And it is going to be fucking glorious." I had personally born witness to the devastation of which certain angels were capable. Deep down, I knew that quiet, unassuming, perpetually cool Logan had that kind of fury within him. I wanted to see him unleash it, preferably at Orion's expense.

He chuckled. "Not anytime soon. Let's go."

Before I could say anything back, he had lifted off, rocketing up into the sky. If I glanced overhead, I could trace the arc of his flight, his shape like a black meteor blocking out the faint sprinkling of stars. He pulled ahead, and I broke into a dead run on the ground. It wasn't a competition, but that didn't mean I'd let him win.

We reached the house in a matter of minutes, at about the same time. Part of me wondered why we had to come back to that place in person when Logan had the ability to break the news with his mind. But he didn't give me time to speculate; I watched him land, climb the steps, and throw open the front door.

"Orion!" The angel's voice resonated in a way I'd never heard. I stepped through the door and glanced at him sidelong. It was beginning to seem as though Logan had been holding out on me, or maybe on all of us. Clearly there was a lot I didn't understand.

"What?" Orion appeared at the top of the stairs, gazing down on us. He was, I thought, exactly where he liked to be, perched above the masses.

His strange, metallic eyes glowed. "What are you doing here?"

Logan pulled no punches. "Veronica is in danger," he said bluntly. "She could be killed."

Orion's gaze immediately sharpened to a razor's edge. I swore the temperature in the whole building dropped by ten degrees. He swept down the stairs, stopping inches from Logan's face.

"Elaborate," he demanded. "Now. Where is she?"

"I believe the wendigo took her," Logan stated serenely. If he was intimidated by the vampire, he gave no indication. "That's all the information I have, and it's almost pure speculation."

"Fuck." Orion's fists and jaw clenched in unison. He turned to me, and for a moment, I prepared for him to lash out. Honestly, I was hoping for it, in a way. His irrational anger would allow me an outlet for the simmering rage I'd been harboring myself.

"She's moving," Logan added. "I don't believe it's voluntary."

Orion grimaced. The wheels turned in his head. I could see him weighing his options against the situation at hand. Finally, he said, "Forget about recovery. Forget about the clan. For now, Veronica is our sole priority."

"Agreed." Logan looked at me. "Seth has made a correct assessment. We need to find her."

"We should be finding her right now," I said. "Who the fuck knows how much time we have?"

Orion nodded. His eyes moved from Logan to me and back again. "What the hell are we standing around for? Let's go get her back."

There was no pushback from him regarding my involvement, no snarky commentary of passive-aggressive digs. The intensity of his focus kind of impressed me, as did his willingness to throw his clan by the wayside, at least temporarily. Did I trust Orion? Absolutely fucking not. But maybe he had a better handle on his priorities than I had first assumed.

For the first time, we were really, truly working together. And it was all for the sake of that damn slayer. The girl who should have tried to kill all of us on sight.

Veronica.

CHAPTER 2

ORION

A thousand thoughts ricocheted through my mind as the three of us stood outside the house on the inlet shore. The fact that Veronica could have been stolen out from under my nose, at a time when she should have been in my charge, filled me with all-consuming rage. With every last fiber of my being, I yearned to destroy until the moment Veronica was returned to my arms.

But as of right now, all threats of destruction lay idle. My attempts to home in on the connection we shared brought back muddled results. All I knew for sure was that she was traveling far and fast. Even the direction was a veiled mystery to me. I feared that soon, she'd be completely out of my reach.

"You said the wendigo took her?" I asked

Logan. Though he claimed his insight was limited, he had spoken his theory with apparent conviction. Suspicion prickled in the back of my mind, but there wasn't time to pull on that loose thread. We couldn't afford to be sidetracked by infighting or divided by long-held grudges. Veronica superseded everything else.

"That's what I think." Logan's perpetual calm threatened to needle its way under my skin, but I forced myself to match it instead of blowing up. He added, "Not much else could carry her so quickly over such a long distance."

Visions of the creature's long, skeletal limbs flashed through my memory, its lanky height towering above my head. I knew he was right, a realization that only sharpened the edge of my anger. As mad as I was that she had been stolen, I also felt an undeniable burden of responsibility.

After all, Veronica was only away from my watch because I had personally failed her. My shortcomings in battle allowed her to be spirited away by another slayer, who was obviously not providing for her in the way I could have. How many precious hours did I lose to recovery following the massacre of my clan? And in what state had Veronica seen me? The idea that she'd witnessed my moments of weakness filled me with an emotion impossible to describe.

Was it shame? Indignance? Vulnerability? I didn't know, but I hated it.

"So what? Are we just gonna stand here like assholes while she's getting carted off to who-knows-where?" Seth demanded.

I jolted back to the present moment and glared at him. "Absolutely not." Then, remembering my pledge to put V above all rivalries, I softened my stance. "You're right. We've wasted enough time."

Logan frowned. "We don't have a plan. It's reasonable to assume that the wendigo has recovered at least some, if not all, of its power. It is not to be underestimated." He glanced at us. "I'm not sure we can find it alone."

I turned my glare on him. "Surely you're not suggesting we have time for a detour. There are three of us, Logan. I should hope we have a fighting chance against one wendigo."

"Yes. If we can *find* it," he repeated pointedly. "This land is vast and largely inhospitable. None of us have a reliable grasp on Veronica's exact location at the current distance. She might be long dead by the time we track the wendigo down."

The silence that fell was tense and heavy. I knew Logan at least had a point. As a slayer,

Veronica rose high above the ranks of her mortal peers. But she still walked among them. Her body housed a beating heart that I feared was more fragile than it seemed. We all feared it, and so we all came to the same reluctant conclusion.

"Fine," Seth burst out suddenly. "So we need some fucking help. Where the hell are we supposed to find *that*?" He turned to me. "Look, man. I don't like being the one to tell you this, but there's no one out there. No one that we found, anyway." He paused. "The clan is gone. You're gonna have to build it from the ground up."

I stared at him. On the surface, those were the typical rash, uninformed words of an outsider, and it irked me to hear him offering any semblance of advice. But deep down, I feared the demon was right. Whatever remained of the clan had probably scattered to the winds in search of safety and a way to bide time until we could recover.

And that meant for now, I was more or less alone.

I grimaced. My wounded pride struggled to recover, though I would never have let him know it. "That isn't how this works," I told Seth curtly. "But if we need to rebuild, we will, no matter how extensive the damage may be."

"Whatever you say," he answered. "We're still

exactly where we started. No V, and no help to get her back. And if we don't make a plan in the next thirty seconds, I'm going after her myself." His eyes blazed with defiance and conviction. A grudging sense of respect welled up in me.

"She'll die if you do that," Logan said simply. He looked at me. "You're not going to like this. But we really only have one choice."

"What's that?" The feeling of being backed into a corner was quickly becoming all too commonplace.

"The other slayer." Logan spoke gravely, as if he knew how severely his words would impact me.

I had braced myself in anticipation of his reply, and yet it still sent me reeling. "No," I growled once I'd recovered my senses. "Absolutely fucking not." There were certain compromises I had to be willing to make in dire times such as these, but working with a man who'd stolen Veronica from me was not one of them.

Logan's days of meek compliance, however, appeared to be over, or at least on hiatus. He didn't flinch as he shook his head. "He's all we have, Orion. More of us against the Wendigo, the better our chances."

Seth gave me no support. "Let's go," he said impatiently. "This is fucking stupid. I'm not fighting you over it. Which is the only time you'll ever hear me say that." He started to walk away, prompting Logan to follow. The threatened loss of my authority was galling, and my instinct was to stop such blatant insubordination at any cost. Then I closed my eyes for a moment and saw Veronica's face floating in the darkness.

Was she hurt? Was she frightened? Was she, as Logan predicted, already dying? I couldn't bear to consider any of those scenarios, and so I too turned and followed Seth away from the house, in the direction of the plush suburb where I had originally located Veronica—and from which she had been taken.

The journey was fast and somber. Logan flew while Seth and I retraced our steps from not too long ago before blazing across the all-too-familiar landscape. I was ever mindful of the dark horizon, knowing that it would eventually give rise to the sun and betray me, as always. Not that the dawn would stop me.

Nothing could have kept me from Veronica. I hoped she knew that. Once more, my mind reached out to hers, and I was dismayed to find that the distance between us had lengthened. A feeling of foreboding descended upon me. I picked up my pace.

Seth glanced over as I drew up alongside him. "Oh, now you're getting serious?" he asked. The remark was devoid of his usual flippancy. "Good."

"When I find that damned creature, I'm going to tear it to shreds," I muttered. There was so much helpless anger boiling in my head and heart. How could this have happened? Where was Veronica being taken? What would happen if we didn't get her back?

"That makes two of us," Seth said. Up above, Logan swooped forward, his great dark wings beating the air. Momentarily, he blocked out the pale eye of the moon, and we were cast in shadow. Seth tilted his head back. He grinned wryly. "Son of a bitch. Some people have all the luck."

The rain-scented wind blew in our faces as we came upon the wide lawn leading up to the house where Veronica had been held. Logan touched down just ahead. I watched his wings fold up and disappear. How strange he appeared in that brief instant, even to my eyes.

Then he approached me and said, "Stay back." As calmly as the command was delivered, I bristled. Who was he to give me orders as if the events of the past few days had changed the very core of who I was?

I drew up to my full height, meeting his cold eyes. "Why?"

Again, Logan didn't flinch. "Because the slayer will kill you on sight," he answered matter-of-factly. "And he can't be blamed for it. Such is his training, after all."

I could almost feel Seth smiling to my right. The spirit of passionate rage inside me yearned to lash out, but I stilled it for Veronica's sake. An invisible clock ticked down, minute by minute. There was no way to know how much time we had left.

"Be quick." I glowered, just to make my displeasure as evident as possible.

He nodded. To Seth, he said, "You stay too. If Orion can't show his face around here, you can't either."

The demon laughed. "That's fair." Logan set off toward the silhouette of the sprawling house in the middle of the lawn, and I saw Seth's face change. He was silent as we faded back into the night to await Logan's return.

The rain in the air began to fall in huge, cold drops. I barely felt it, barely felt anything other than the burning desire to find Veronica, sweep her into my arms, and never let her ago.

It was, I suspected, a sentiment the three of us

had somehow come to share. The suspicion gnawed at my bones. I pushed it down. Veronica belonged to me—and yet I'd failed to save her on my own. Could I truly claim her in the face of the weakness I'd exhibited?

I clenched my teeth. This hunt for the wendigo would be one of vengeance and redemption, through which I would once again prove myself worthy. And as soon as I had her back by my side, the reconstruction of the Anchorage clan could begin in earnest.

CHAPTER 3

VERONICA

It was the cold that woke me up, the kind of cold that slices straight to the bone and seems to freeze from the inside out. My skin felt like a layer of frost was forming on the surface, tiny crystals of ice crackling with every movement. I blinked against a current of fierce wind. Around my face, my hair flew in wild pink tangles.

Goddamn, I'm never going to be able to brush these out. That was my first groggy thought, as I tried to stretch my aching arms and legs. The back of my neck and shoulders hurt too, and I realized I'd been completely limp for who knew how long, suspended by my torso in the air. And then the memories came rushing back, and I knew where I was and what had happened.

"Oh, shit," I murmured. "How the hell am I gonna get out of this one?"

The wendigo had picked up speed while I was out. I looked down and saw the ground flying by beneath my dangling feet in a blur of white and gray and brown. We were no longer surrounded by the same dense cover of trees. The air smelled fresh, biting at the inside of my mouth and nose. Was it my imagination, or had the temperature plummeted since I passed out?

Squinting my eyes against the frigid air, I glared up at the wendigo. "I wish you had fur, you bastard. Then I might at least be warm." It paid me no mind at all as it galloped through a gently rolling, surprisingly open patch of land. Finally, the horizon caught my eye, and I let out a gasp that was snatched away on the wind.

The jagged blue peaks of the Alaska Range jutted from the earth, rising like great gems into the sky. They went as far as I could see, but the crown jewel stood directly in our path—Denali. Shocked and struck dumb by its sheer majesty, my jaw fell open. I had some vague recollection of knowing that this was where we were ultimately headed, but I had never seen the mountain in person.

Now I was barreling toward it at breakneck

speed, in the grasp of an otherworldly death monster. Not exactly how I imagined my first visit to the sacred peak might go. Again, I wondered what the wendigo hoped to achieve by bringing me north to Denali. It had to have a plan because there was no slowing down. The world around me was a dizzying blur, except when I managed to catch a glimpse of the sky. Toward the east, the stars were beginning to fade into slowly lightening shades of blue and purple.

Soon it would be sunrise. I could hardly believe enough time had passed that another day was about to dawn. Wasn't I literally just tucked safely into the guest room at Lian's house, fresh off a clandestine rendezvous with Seth? Hadn't I just begged him to save Orion's life, much to his displeasure?

Funny how fast things were changing in my life. The wendigo lifted its arm, rocketing me high into the air. I held on to its bony fingers for dear life. Behind us, the great swath of land that we'd traveled spread out in the direction of Anchorage, two hundred miles or more. The distance was daunting, to say the least.

How long would it take for Orion, Seth, and Logan to find me, assuming they were all looking? And if I somehow managed to get out of this shitshow on my own, how long would it take me to find my way back?

An anxious foreboding hung palpably over my head like the clouds cloaking the top of the mountain.

It was getting harder to see where we were headed. My vantage point became a blur of cold fog, wet snow, and bursts of ice and rock that cascaded down every time the wendigo dug its claws into the mountain face. I shielded myself as best I could, but in no time, I was soaked. The howling wind whipped my hair and clothes stiff, scratching at my limbs and face.

Inside my body, my heart still beat strong. All things considered, I didn't feel too cold. If there was any time I had ever been particularly grateful for my slayer blood, it was right then. The wendigo bounded upward, scaling the cliffs as though they were paved pathways.

I squeezed my eyes shut tight. Ice melted off my eyelashes, running down my cheeks like pure, salt-less tears. Nothing good would come of me accidentally drying my eyeballs out when the final destination was rapidly becoming clear. The wendigo, in all its fury, was headed straight for the peak of Mt. Denali. We were only going one direction now, and that was *up*.

The air grew thinner every minute. At first, as I became aware that it was getting harder to draw breath, I instinctually wanted to panic. The irrational desire was to claw more oxygen out of the air, or to open my lungs as wide as they would go. Certain kinds of mortal danger I knew how to face with a confident smile on my face. Fighting vamps? Sure. Wrangling werewolves? No problem. Suffocating on the side of a mountain, mid-ascent?

If I got the wendigo to drop me now, assuming I didn't immediately fall to my death off a sheer ledge, I'd be stranded in the middle of absolute nowhere, exposed to the elements, strong, but not invincible. Death would be agonizingly slow, my suffering great.

On the other hand, if I decided to let things play out according to the wendigo's half-baked plans, I might still end up dead or captive for an indeterminate amount of time.

I pressed my lips together. "They've gotta be searching for me by now, right?" I imagined Orion, wild-eyed and full of anger, Seth smoldering with ill-suppressed rage, and Logan, so cool and calm. The three of them had fought constantly in the days leading up to the present disaster. Could they really pull their shit together long enough to work as a team?

I hoped so. God, I hoped so. But I knew better than to count on it.

Suddenly, the wendigo coiled its haunches and leapt across one last crevasse. I made the mistake of glancing downward as we sailed from edge to edge, into a narrow, bottomless maw that went from white, to blue, to black. The knot already forming in my stomach tightened. I forced in another breath.

Then the gloom that had wrapped us so tightly in its arms receded all at once, like the tide moments before a tsunami. I looked up to see a brilliant plane of crystalline white snow, flooded by the light of a brand-new sunrise. For an instant, it was impossible to distinguish Denali from the edge of the sky. My heart stuttered in my chest.

The spell was broken when my field of view changed, and I realized the wendigo was putting me down. As my feet touched solid ground for the first time in hours, I almost fell to my knees. Arms out, flailing for balance, I staggered through unmarked drifts of snow. The pajamas I had borrowed from Lian stuck to my skin, drenched through with ice water.

One of the things I had always been taught as a slayer was never to turn my back on the enemy. That morning, on the peak of Denali, I made a rookie mistake. The wendigo couldn't have been out of my sight for more than twenty or thirty seconds, but that was more than long enough to grant it the upper hand. Later, I'd be ashamed to admit I never saw it coming. The last thing I remembered was the line between earth and sky coming back into focus.

Then my vision sank down into blackness. I had the surreal sensation of falling, although I never felt an impact.

Oh, fuck, I thought. *Not this again.*

CHAPTER 4

LOGAN

The house glowed, casting shadows from the lights in the windows as I walked up the front path. It should have been warm and inviting, a symbol of luxury and prestige, nestled in the embrace of the most upscale neighborhood in the city. Instead, tension radiated from every beam. The windows watched me like baleful yellow eyes.

I could sense two people inside. Their energy was fraught with worry, one more than the other. There was anger, frustration, and betrayal mixed in with desperate concern. They too seemed to understand the gravity of Veronica's plight, for which I was thankful. We had no extra minutes to spend on explanations.

The door swung open almost before I finished

knocking. The slayer stood in the entryway, blocking access to the house. He was tall, blond, and broad-shouldered; up close, I could see exactly why Orion detested him. The man was too confident, too powerful—and too suspicious of anyone like us.

He examined me carefully, poised for action. Behind him, I caught a glimpse of a young woman who was not Veronica but had been in her company before. Traces of Veronica's energy remained entangled with hers. I knew she was the one I needed to talk to if I wanted any hope of pleading my case, but that was not going to happen. The slayer kept her back.

"What do you want?" He squared his stance and folded his arms. I glanced at the girl. "Hey. I'm not going to ask twice."

Her gaze flicked uneasily toward him. "Trent."

The ice was obviously very thin and growing thinner by the second. I decided to be as direct as possible. "I need help."

Briefly, something other than guarded wariness flickered across his face. "That's interesting." He stepped across the threshold. "I'm listening. For now."

I gave no indication that Orion and Seth were there. My strongest chances of success hinged on two things: civility, and the appearance of neutrality. My companions weren't proficient in either of those.

"I need to find Veronica. She's in danger." At this, I noticed the girl perked up, suddenly invested.

She came forward. "What did you say?"

Gently, Trent placed his hand on her arm. "Give me one reason to trust you," he demanded. He stared through me as if he knew exactly who and what I was. "Do you know where Veronica is?"

"Not exactly." I took a deep breath. "That's why I'm here. She's moving fast, and I can't track her on my own."

He frowned. "I suppose you thought I wouldn't know you brought your friends along." He looked over my left shoulder, then my right. "They're not so great at staying hidden. Like you told them to."

The jig, or whatever we thought it had been, was up. I sighed and raised my hands, palms out, in a gesture of supplication. "We couldn't afford to make the wrong impression right off the bat," I said. "Are you saying you would *not* have gone straight for Orion's throat? Because I'm not sure I believe that."

"It's pretty ballsy of any of you to show your faces here again," Trent murmured. "Especially him." He moved another step closer to me. I held my ground. "You really want to help Veronica? Maybe she doesn't need weirdos like you screwing things up for her. Have you ever thought of that?"

Actually, I had. Many times, in fact. Pervasive self-doubt was one of the unfortunate hallmarks of the fallen, doomed as we were to question ourselves and our actions for all eternity. But I didn't say it out loud.

The girl interrupted. "Trent! We don't have time for this." She gripped his arm, her eyes boring into him. "Veronica's *gone*. If they have a lead, we have to take it." She paused. "Please." Her voice broke on the word.

I looked at her once more, and a wave of desperate sorrow broke almost violently over me. She was steeped in true fear for her friend, the kind that made her willing to take certain risks. Trent looked at her too, and a current of love swept across his aura. He softened a little, though not enough to back down.

"What have you got?" he asked brusquely. "And tell the others to show themselves. I'd rather we were all on semi-equal footing from the start, if we're really going to do this."

The girl kept her gaze trained on me as I signaled for the vampire and the demon to come up to the porch. I felt genuinely sorry for her, not just the condescending pity of a supernatural toward a fragile, mortal woman. She embodied the helplessness we were all fighting.

"I promise I am here to help," I told her.

She nodded. "I know." The slayer seemed not to like her stubborn confidence, but he chose, perhaps wisely, not to say anything. We were all silent while Orion and Seth flanked my position. Predictably, Orion was focused solely on the slayer, whom I was sure he viewed as his nemesis.

"The wendigo took her," I began once everyone had found their place. It was Trent's turn to nod. His distrust, particularly of Orion, showed plainly on his countenance, but he listened. "It appears to be running directly north, toward the mountains, at an alarming rate of speed."

"Toward the mountains?" Trent furrowed his brow. He and the girl exchanged a puzzled glance, and then his expression cleared. "The national park," he muttered. "That goddamned thing is taking her to Denali."

"What does that mean?" the girl interjected. "Is there something up there?"

"I don't know, but we're going to find out. Can you get us a car, babe?" Trent brushed past me while he spoke to her. He was suddenly all business, thinly veiled animosity aside. "Not all of us can fly like this one here."

I followed him down the porch stairs. Orion and Seth closed in on each side. Orion had yet to take his eyes off Trent for even a second. "I won't go ahead," I told them. "Nothing good can come of splitting us up right now." It would be a dream come true for the wendigo to pick us off one by one.

"Take the car in the garage," the girl called after us. "And drive like hell."

But we had barely made it ten feet from the house when I sensed the faint trill of Veronica's energy waver and go silent. Surveying the faces around me, I saw very quickly that I was not the only one. We froze in our tracks, none of us breathing. No eye contact was made.

"Oh, shit," Seth whispered. Without missing another beat, he broke into a dead run toward the garage. Orion and Trent did the same. I would have too, but the girl stopped me. She'd come down from the house upon seeing that something was wrong.

"What happened?" Her grip on my shoulder was surprisingly unrelenting, finely manicured nails digging into my flesh like claws. "Don't even think about lying to me." She had turned from scared to fierce in the blink of an eye.

Her strength compelled me to tell her the truth, as raw as it was. Far in the distance, I felt no trace of Veronica anymore—and since she was still a mortal, that could only mean one thing. I looked Veronica's friend in her sharp dark eyes.

"She's dead. Just now. I'm sorry."

All the color drained from the girl's face. She staggered backward, releasing my shoulder. Her hands flew to cover her mouth. "What?" she breathed. "No. Oh my God, no!" I saw her sway, and I thought she might faint, but by some Herculean feat of inner strength, she managed to remain upright. "That can't be. You have to have made a mistake."

I shook my head. "There's no mistake. She's become unmoored, drifting between realms. No longer present on the mortal plane." What I didn't voice was the depth of my own regret, nor my determination to somehow make things right. I wasn't sure she'd understand.

The girl stared at me, furious and heartbroken. "Fix this," she whispered. "I don't know how, and I don't care. Bring her back."

I said, "I will. I swear." A few tears leaked from

the corners of her eyes, which she angrily wiped away.

"I'll hold you to it," she answered.

Orion's voice broke through the gravity of the pact we had just made. "Logan! Get moving!" Without another word, I left her standing on the front path in front of her house, gazing after me as I ran for the car.

CHAPTER 5

SETH

We peeled out of there with the slayer behind the wheel. Logan got the front seat because his sense for V appeared to be the strongest at the moment, which left Orion and me to brood together in the back. Neither of us were particularly pleased with the arrangement, but we had little choice.

"Is there no way to travel faster?" the vamp demanded. "Veronica's life is hanging in the balance!"

"No, it isn't," Logan said. "Her spirit has passed fully through the veil. She's departed from the mortal realm. Her body is just a vessel now."

Orion fell silent. He had gone uncharacteristically pale, even for him. The tension in his neck and jaw was visible. "How long?" he finally growled. "How long to get to her?"

The slayer glanced in the rearview mirror. The car's engine revved as he caught our eyes and we shot forward down the road. "Not too long, I hope. But I'm gonna need you to strap in if you don't want to be left behind. We're not stopping if you fly out the rear windshield."

It was a joy I didn't know I needed to see Orion so angry and unable to do anything about it. He buckled his seatbelt with unnecessary force, and I had to suppress the urge to laugh. Honestly, at that point it was hard not to feel at least a little bad for the guy—who would have thought he'd go from king of the city to the back seat of a borrowed car in a matter of a few days? I was willing to bet not even Logan had fallen quite that hard.

"You're sure she was moving north?" Trent spoke over the roar of the engine as we sped along the quiet neighborhood road. Dawn had broken not long before, and the whole scene lay bathed in tranquil golden light. Hard to believe we were on our way to pry Veronica's wandering spirit back from the jaws of death.

"Yes." Logan paused. "A straight path. Purposeful. The wendigo knows where it's going."

"Hmm." Trent frowned. "That, or it's being

drawn there for some reason. Either way, not good." The speedometer needle inched toward the far right side of the dial. The manicured neighborhood streets gave way to a highway that was just as empty. And we sat confined in the car like kids who'd gotten in trouble for fighting. As if we were being shipped off to prison, or military school.

"Hey, Logan," I said, mostly to break the silence. "How's this compare to flying?"

He chuckled. "It doesn't." Then to Trent, he said, "That's not a statement on your driving."

Trent's stony façade cracked a little. He smirked. "I appreciate the clarification." The temporary easing of tension was strange, but also welcome. I didn't like feeling as though we were piloting a hearse down the road at a hundred miles an hour, trying to head off a funeral. "You okay back there?" Trent asked. He was talking to Orion more than me.

Orion replied with little more than a sullen glare. He despised his lack of control nearly as much as the fact that Trent was the one who had taken over. "When Veronica is found," he said, "she is mine. No talks. No compromises. I'm taking her with me."

Trent's laughter carried an edge. "The hell you are, my friend." He turned back to the road. The engine surged. Outside the window, the world leapt by in a blur. "We'll be there in an hour," he said. "Maybe a little more."

I could tell Orion wanted to throw him out of the car. He gripped the seat so hard his knuckles stood out under his skin. Every so often, his eyes would dart around nervously, as if he expected something or someone to leap from the trunk or onto the windshield.

I bore it for as long as I could stand, and when I ran out of patience, I let him know. "Cut it out, man. You're making me fucking paranoid."

Orion stared at me. His voice was low and tight. "Need I remind you that we are inside of a car with the very same slayer who took it upon himself to remove Veronica from the sacred grove? It is still all too possible that we allowed ourselves to be played for fools, Seth. Even you." He stopped, presumably to let his words sink in. "Especially you."

I frowned. "What? Why especially me? What the hell is that supposed to mean?" I had to admit that I liked this new version of Orion even less than before.

"Because you're letting your guard down," Orion hissed. "You're trusting him. I can tell. And he might be leading all of us directly into a trap."

I rolled my eyes. "Blow it out your ass, Orion. You're here too, aren't you?" I gestured toward the driver's seat. "Listen, if this guy turns out to be a double-crossing prick, we'll kill him as soon as he betrays us. Just like that. No problem. Three of us, one of him." I raised my eyebrows. "Unless you're scared of him and that's what this is really about."

The vamp bristled. "Of course not." Out of the corner of my eye, I saw the edge of Trent's mouth twitch upward.

"Fine. Then it shouldn't be a big fucking deal." I leaned back against the upholstery and ran my fingers through my hair. "You're losing it without V around, man. A couple more hours of this and you'll be a stark, raving lunatic."

Orion grumbled, but he didn't deny it. He tried to maintain an expression of cold neutrality, but his face kept shifting, the veil peeling back on his emotions. I imagined that the man sitting beside me in that car was the real Orion—or maybe it was whoever he had been before making the transition to the night. Losing Veronica had clearly altered him in ways he barely understood.

"I need her back," he said softly. "No matter the cost."

"That makes four of us," I agreed. "Five, if you count the girl we left at the house."

"The way I feel for Veronica is beyond anything you could possibly understand," Orion declared. He sat up straighter, puffing out his chest. Finally, he'd found something to be smug and condescending about, which returned him closer to his natural, insufferable state. "She's destined to be mine."

Why was I relieved to hear him acting like a total dickhead again? *Don't tell me you were concerned about the guy,* I scolded myself with disgust. The idea of caring about him repulsed me. *Don't forget he would've left your corpse to freeze in the Underworld until the end of time.*

Still, every time I looked at or thought about Orion now, all I could see was the way Veronica had looked at me as she begged me to save his life. Of all the mortal opinions in the world, hers was the one I listened to most. And she obviously saw something in that pompous horror show, so I had somehow begun to entertain the idea that he might not be utterly useless.

Not that Orion would ever know I thought of him as anything other than an undead sack of air. And I had an important question for him. "What if other people were to challenge you for her?"

He narrowed his eyes. "They would fail," came the answer.

"Oh, it's that simple?" I kept an eye on the back of Logan's head in an attempt to gauge his reaction, but the son of a bitch never turned around.

"Yes." Orion lifted his head defiantly. "It is."

"Can I ask you something?" Trent drove with one hand now, although he hadn't slowed so much as a mile an hour. He guided the car down the highway with the deftness of a professional.

Grudgingly, Orion asked, "What is it?"

"Why do you talk about Veronica like she's a possession instead of a person? Something tells me she wouldn't be happy to hear you speaking like you own her."

The vampire's temper flared. "I can talk about her any way I please," he snarled. "These are rich words coming from a man who slung her over his shoulder and dashed off like a coward!"

"But I did that to save her life," Trent answered calmly. "She was unconscious, man. And so were you. Someone had to get her out of there."

Orion was angrily quiet for a few moments. "Veronica accepts me as I am," he countered. "If I have flaws, they don't affect my love for her."

"*If* you have flaws?" I burst out, unable to resist. "Come on, Orion. A perfect person wouldn't have gotten laid out by a wendigo."

"Nor would he have gotten captured and

banished from the realm," Orion shot back. Then he turned to face the window. "Nonetheless, you are correct. I have failed in many ways in such a short time. It is a disgrace to my clan."

His candid admission caught me off guard. One thing I had never expected from Orion was humbleness, or any amount of vulnerability. Perhaps he was finally adjusting to his new position at the bottom of the totem pole, however temporary it turned out to be.

"Hey, no sweat," I said. "We're all a fucking disgrace in one way or another. That's how we ended up crammed in this damn car together." I jerked my thumb toward the driver. "Besides him, I guess."

Trent shook his head, smiling wryly. "No, no. Me too."

"See?" I reached over and patted Orion on the shoulder. "You're not special, boss."

He didn't answer.

CHAPTER 6

VERONICA

The first thing I noticed was that the gnawing, ravenous cold was gone, and so was the wind. In its place lay the heaviest silence I had ever heard in my life. The still air was thick with it, a palpable hush. It reminded me, bizarrely, of attending a funeral where the deceased was too young and no one had anything to say.

Little did I know how much, or how soon, that wayward thought would come back to haunt me.

Slowly, I got to my feet. All my senses were on high alert, but there was nothing to sense. I'd never been in a place so completely devoid of life and sound. Despite everything I had learned over years of slayer training and field experience, I knew I wasn't prepared for whatever the hell this was.

"Where is this place?" Of course, there was no one to answer, but I felt better hearing a voice, any voice, even if it was just my own. I started to step carefully through the pitch blackness, and as my eyes adjusted, silhouettes began to emerge from the dark. I drew a sharp breath. Every muscle in my body tensed. They were humanoid shadows, and they were moving toward me.

Quickly, I felt for my staff. The cold hand of dread gripped my stomach; I didn't have anything other than the clothes on my back. Unarmed but undaunted, I clenched my hands into fists. *No weapon, no problem.*

But the shadows never seemed to take notice of me or get too close. They just shambled by at a distance, staring blankly ahead. And they didn't seem to be...real? No, that wasn't it. They were real like clouds were real, or steam on the surface of a mirror. I could almost see right through them.

"Okay, I don't know what the hell is going on," I muttered, "but I don't like it." Not that my personal preferences really mattered in this situation. Looking over my shoulder, I saw only the backs of the ghostly figures who had passed me, and nothing else except infinite blackness. There was nothing to do besides move forward.

So I kept on wading through the void, waiting

for something to happen. The farther I went, the more people I saw, until there was almost a silent, shuffling crowd. Everything was shaded in grays and whites, and I wondered half-jokingly if I'd gotten trapped in some kind of old-time purgatory.

Then I saw it, cutting through the gloom like sunlight breaking through fog—a flash of normal color. Was I finally reaching the end of this bizarre dream world? Was it even a dream? Cautious excitement rushed through my body. The last thing I wanted was to be stuck in a nowhere dimension while there was a wendigo on the loose in Alaska.

As I picked up my pace, the slow-moving throng of spirits shifted, creating a rough path before me. I looked up. The air caught in my lungs. My heart skipped at least one beat, if not several. It took a minute or two to find my voice, and when I did, it came out as barely more than a whisper.

"Dylan?"

He glanced toward me at the sound of his name. For a moment, he appeared to be as surprised as I was, but the shock rapidly melted into the same smile I remembered: an almost shy grin that crossed his face halfway at a time. His eyes, green like emeralds, were bright in the dim ambience.

Weren't they blue before?

I dismissed the stray thought as nonsensical babbling from a blindsided mind. Dylan had made regular appearances in my dreams for a while, but I never thought I'd actually get to see my ex-boyfriend again after he'd been killed by the vampires. Although I was thrilled beyond words, I found myself frozen in place, afraid he'd disappear if I moved. After his death, I wished for such a moment so much that it hurt. I cried, hated myself, blamed myself for not saving him… so to see him brought back all the broken emotions.

Then he said, "Hey, Veronica. You just gonna stand there?" And he sounded the same as he always had. Like no time had passed at all.

By the time I reached him, tears had spilled down my cheeks. I reached out and put my hands on his arms. Unlike the others, he was solid beneath my touch, so warm and real.

"I can't believe it's really you," I said.

His grin widened. "Me neither. C'mere." Dylan put his arms around me, and a part of my heart that had been frozen since his death immediately melted. I buried my face in his shoulder. He squeezed tight. We stayed that way for a long moment, as everything about touching him came back, how well I fit into his arms, how his breath always warmed my ear, and even his woodsy smell with a hint of vanilla lingered. My breath hitched all the way down to my lungs to be in his arms again.

I'd missed him so much.

Cried even more.

So I cherished that silent moment.

After a few moments, I pulled back and took a deep breath. "I thought you were dead. I mean, you are dead."

The grin faded a little. "Yeah, I am. And I hate to break it to you, but uh…you are too."

I blinked. "What?"

Dylan shrugged. "You must be if you're here." He gestured to the space around us. "Look at this place. It's not exactly for the living."

He was right, and I had known it on some level as soon as I opened my eyes, but the truth was hard to wrap my head around. "Huh." I frowned. "I guess that son of a bitch really killed me."

Dylan offered a wry smile. "Happens to the best of us. But there are upsides. One, I get to be with you again, and two, I think I know a way out."

The sweetness of his first sentence was overshadowed by the strangeness of his second. I stared at him. "How is that possible? You just said we're dead."

"Yeah, but that's the thing. It's not supposed to be like this. You know, this walking around, having conversations, existing together. I used to be alone, isolated from every other being I ever saw, no matter how many others there were. We couldn't speak to each other, couldn't hear anything, couldn't touch. But then I woke up."

I hesitated. An odd little seedling of doubt began to grow in the back of my mind. "What does that mean, you 'woke up'?"

Dylan looked at me, then looked away. "I can't really explain it," he said. "It's like everything came back into my world. All the color, all the feeling. The memories." His eyes returned to my face. "You."

Those tiny, whispering doubts didn't quite go away. But it was kind of easy to push them down while he was standing in front of me. How many times had I dreamt of this exact moment, asleep and awake? Whatever crazy opportunity had just fallen into my lap, I couldn't pass it up.

"Maybe we'll worry about the details later," I told him. "What's your plan?"

"This is going to sound insane, but hear me out." He nodded toward the nothingness stretching out forever in every direction. "I'm pretty sure we just keep walking and a door will appear somewhere."

I smirked. "That's your genius-level strategy?"

"Hey, I didn't say it was genius-level," he shot back, smiling. "That was all you." Dylan reached over and took my hand. "Come on. We might as well give it a shot, right? Not like either of us has anything better going on."

He had a solid point, and I loved the feel of his hand in mine, so I decided it couldn't hurt to go along for the ride. "All right. Lead the way."

We walked in silence for a few steps, each of us lost in our own thoughts. I kept wondering if this whole thing was some kind of cold-induced hallucination, brought on by the frigid peak of Denali. Or maybe the things I had always heard about the mountain's mystic sacredness were true, and I was on a spiritual quest—embodied by my dead ex-boyfriend.

I frowned slightly. Dylan raised an eyebrow.

"What's up?" he asked.

"Nothing." I shook my head.

"I guess this is weird, huh?" He chuckled. "It's weird for me too, but in a good way. A great way, actually. This is like, everything I ever imagined it would be." He squeezed my hand. "I can't stop thinking about how damn lucky I am to get a second chance at a future with you. You were always my dream girl, V."

I felt the blush creeping up into my cheeks before he finished talking. Even if they were nothing more than words, his sweet nothings filled a space I'd never really noticed. As much as I adored and craved my current cast of men, none of them spent an undue amount of time on compliments or optimism. I had really committed to the dramatic, mercurial, sometimes-strong-and-silent aesthetic.

Which meant being with Dylan was a breath of fresh air cleansing my spirit. Suddenly, it stopped mattering where we were. I could almost envision our old life, the way things had been back in Seattle. No bloody gang wars, no danger lurking around every corner, no sitting up at night waiting to see if he'd make it home. There was only the incomparable feeling of being young and in love.

But as quickly as the nostalgia appeared, it began to curdle and fade. I simply could not allow myself to toss aside the experience I'd had since Dylan's death in favor of rose-tinted glasses. A twinge of skepticism still needled at me, not least because the door he mentioned had yet to materialize. What if he was a figment of my imagination, a specter born of loneliness and grief?

Gently, I took my hand away. "That's sweet of you to say," I murmured.

Dylan slowed his pace. "Well, it's true." His expression turned apprehensive. "Listen, I know this is all strange, believe me. And I'm not asking you to take everything I say as pure gospel. But I promise it's me. I've never been able to lie to you about anything."

"Where's the door?" I stopped walking.

"I don't know." He looked genuinely perplexed. "I feel like it should be here any minute now." He took a few steps forward uncertainly.

"Is it possible we're both being lied to?" I asked.

He answered readily. "Sure it is."

His candor somehow managed to set me at ease and make me nervous at the same time. My heart wanted to accept him unquestioningly, but my head wasn't totally on board. I watched him while he wasn't gazing straight at me, and I noted his eyes again—green as summer grass. And yet, I could have sworn they were blue.

Weren't they?

"Look!" Dylan pointed to a spot in the formless dark. "There!" A spark had been kindled, and as we observed from a distance, it began to grow. Gradually, outlined in light, the shape of a portal began to emerge. I shielded my eyes.

"Is that—?"

Dylan broke out into a grin. "It's the door. It's gotta be! I can see something on the other side!" He ran for it. "Veronica, c'mon! I have no idea how long it will stay open!"

He was already halfway to the opening before I made my feet move. On the surface, the choice seemed more than obvious: Follow Dylan, reclaim the life I thought I lost years ago, ride off into the sunset, and live happily ever after.

But even then, I knew things were going to be far from easy. After all, there were at least three people waiting on the other side of that doorway who wouldn't be so happy to see a man I had once loved.

CHAPTER 7

ORION

I had never been so happy to be out in the bitter, bone-aching cold. The ascent of Denali was a grueling, unforgiving trek, even for those of us who had come out on the other side of death. This was a cold that cut through all layers of mysticism, reducing us to equal vessels of misery.

Still, nobody complained. We were all grateful to be free of the confines of Trent's vehicle, which sat temporarily abandoned somewhere in the foothills. With our combined powers, it was faster to tackle the mountain on foot, although Logan didn't dare fly in the face of the slicing wind. I had intended to try and lose the slayer at the earliest convenience, but to my chagrin, he kept up remarkably well.

He also seemed to be fully aware of my schemes. "You disappointed, vamp?" he asked, cracking a grim smile. Despite the way in which he had softened a bit during the excruciating ride north, his eyes remained cold and calculating. I didn't trust him at all.

"That is not the way I would prefer you to address me," I informed him. There were a lot of things I did not prefer about him, to be frank. He was strong, fast, and surefooted as we raced over treacherous terrain, our footsteps sending sparkling showers of snow and ice down into bottomless ravines. I wanted to think it'd be easy to push him over the edge, but that was a fight I couldn't afford to pick at the moment.

Not because I feared that I would lose. Because of what it could cost Veronica.

The air grew thinner as we climbed, and every time I looked up, I saw the clear, hard blue of the sky stretching on forever. It was little wonder that the mountain was thought of as a holy place, rich in magic and secrets. I had to admit that if the veil was going to be thin anywhere, it might as well be here.

Logan was the first to reach the summit. He paused ahead of us and glanced back. "Brace yourselves," he warned in his quiet, solemn voice. "I'm not sure what we'll find."

"Keep going," I ordered. "I don't care."

Moments later, I ate my words. The four of us stood at what seemed like the top of the entire world, staring down at Veronica's body. The silence was deafening. Out of the corner of my eye, I saw the snow and ice melting at Seth's feet, streaming off the cliff face and down into oblivion. He steamed with rage.

I fought the urge to drop to my knees. The pain was a knife to the heart, a hammer to the ribs. How incredible that a physical sensation I hadn't fully felt in years still had the power to fell me. Though I didn't breathe, I found myself gasping.

"How could this happen? How?" The voice was barely recognizable as my own.

"Fuck." Anguished, Seth let out a roar to the uncaring sky. "Fuck! We're too fucking late!" His furious gaze swept around the semicircle, searching for someone or something to blame.

"Maybe not," Logan said. "She looks like she's sleeping. I can feel it. That could be a good sign."

I stared at him. "What can we do? Tell me."

"I don't fucking care what it is," Seth added. "You want me to obliterate this whole fucking mountain, I'll do it. I'm ready. Let's go."

The angel held out a hand. "No. Calm down." He closed his eyes for a moment that felt like an hour. "She's likely on the other side of the veil somewhere, wandering. Like I said, adrift. Unanchored."

"Not helpful, angel-boy," Seth growled. "How do we get her back?"

Logan didn't answer right away. It was the slayer who stepped in with an answer. "We may need to go in after her. I don't see signs of the wendigo anywhere, which means her body will likely stay safe while we're searching."

"Okay, so let's go." Seth stepped toward Logan, and I was quick to follow. "I don't know why the fuck we're standing around here with our thumbs up our asses. 'Cause I'm willing to bet her fragile mortal spirit isn't supposed to stay wherever she is for too long, right? Isn't that how this bullshit usually works?"

"Yes." Logan frowned. "I think it would be fairly easy to open a pathway from here. But it could be disastrous for some of us." He turned to me. "And by that I mean you, Orion. Since you're technically already dead, I have no idea what will happen once you step across the veil."

My response took no thinking whatsoever. "It

doesn't matter. I will sacrifice every iota of my being for her. Open the path." Never had I spoken such undiluted, heartfelt truth. The occasion would have been auspicious under any other circumstances.

"You heard the man," Seth barked. "Get us through there. We'll deal with the consequences later." His eyes, blazing with anger and passion, met mine just long enough for him to give a nod of acknowledgement, perhaps also of thanks. Much as I tended to despise him, the joint loss of Veronica had kindled an unspoken bond between us. If nothing else, we were united in our efforts to save her.

"Agreed," said the slayer. "There's no time left."

Logan didn't hesitate any longer. He reached out his hand again, seeming to lay the palm flat against the air. His entire being glowed, channels of energy running like blood through veins throughout his body. The wind around us picked up to a cutting howl. As I watched the place where the fabric of the mortal realm began to rend apart, I held my breath.

But there was no explosion, no grand entrance or exit. The rift was there, but it was small, and it grew at a snail's pace. Each passing minute blew away in the miasma of snow whirling past. I waited until I couldn't physically bear it any longer.

"Logan!" I bellowed. "Let me through!" Engaged as he was in the opening of the path, Logan was powerless to stop me, although he saw me coming. "I'll rip the veil apart myself!"

"No!" The slayer lunged into my path, striking out at the center of my chest. The blow sent me staggering backward, but not for long. I put my head and shoulders down and charged him like a bull, completely intent on tossing him to his death if that was what it took. Not a single person in the universe could have kept me from Veronica.

"Get out of my way!" The words were stolen from my mouth by the howling wind. Trent grappled the brunt of my charge, locking his arm around the back of my neck and shoulder. I felt the power coursing through him, bestowed, as mine was, by some supernatural force. It was as if he had been placed there by divine intervention to stop me.

"Don't be an asshole," he shouted. "Logan is doing exactly what you told him to do. If you fuck this up now, our chances of finding Veronica shrink down to almost nothing. Hell, I don't even know if you'd survive long enough to see her again." He shoved me back. "Stand there, keep your goddamn mouth shut, and wait. There's nothing else we can do."

Seth caught me and set me on my feet. He glowered over my shoulder at the slayer, death in his demon eyes. "You motherfucker," he snarled. "You'd be fucking dead if I didn't know you were right."

I rounded on Seth. "This is bullshit. We don't have time for this!"

"You think the path between realms gives a shit about how much time we have?" Trent demanded. He gestured at the rift, which had widened slowly but surely. "This is the only way to keep it stable. Otherwise we have no way of knowing where we'll end up once we go through. Look, this is one thing you know absolutely nothing about, all right? Trust me. You need to swallow your vampire pride and let other people take point."

"He's right," Seth added. "As much as it fucking pains me to say."

I opened my mouth to argue, but before I could get any words out, a strange sensation washed over me. I threw back my head. Except for the squall Logan had kicked up, the sky remained empty, bright blue.

Then why could I sense a dark cloud passing

through? In my mind's eye, it was a towering thunderhead, a herald of chaos and doom. And it was accompanied by foreboding so heavy it was nearly tangible. The very air at the peak of the mountain changed from barely there to thick and suffocating.

All of us felt it. The bickering ceased immediately. We exchanged glances. The slayer was the first to look toward the opening Logan continued to forge. That was when I began to suspect there was something wrong. The weight that I was feeling, that threatened to crush me into nothing, emanated from the path. I strained to see through to the other side.

"Logan—" I called. My yearning for Veronica had not subsided, but suddenly I was wary of the things that might be lurking beyond.

"Don't talk to him," Trent said. "It's too late. We have to let it happen." In the past few seconds, his confidence had turned into resignation. We all sensed a drastic shift, but none of us could name it.

"What the fuck just happened?" Seth grew wild-eyed. "What did you do, Logan?" It was his turn to be stopped by Trent, who wrangled the demon back into position.

"It wasn't Logan. Keep your cool." But Trent's gaze was glued to the ever-widening path now.

Then a flash of cruelly bright light erased my vision. I flinched away instinctively, protecting as much of my body as possible. The light carried with it a burst of energy, within which I picked out Veronica's very strongly. My soul leapt for joy—until I realized that she wasn't alone.

There was someone else with her. No, not just with her, *entwined* in her aura. Someone whose energy she gravitated toward in a way that did not please me. As the light subsided, my eyes refocused, and I saw two figures step forward from the place where the path had been. Belatedly, I noticed Veronica's body had disappeared from our feet.

She was beaming as she came toward us, harsh sunlight reflecting off her lustrous pink hair. In that moment, she was the most beautiful being in the universe, across all realms. I forgot everything in my burning desire to hold her in my arms.

Yet, indeed, she was not alone. My face darkened as I became aware of the companion she had acquired on the other side of the veil. He was a young man, perhaps her age in mortal years, or perhaps more, if he happened to be one of us.

I instantly disliked him, partially because the first thing he did was grab on to Veronica's hand. But there was also an imbalance in his manner and energy, subtle enough that I couldn't quite pinpoint the problem. All I knew for sure was that I wanted to send him straight back to wherever he had come from. And then I wanted to seal the path between the realms—for good.

CHAPTER 8

SETH

"Who the hell is that?" I said to no one in particular. If there was one thing I hadn't expected out of this situation, it was for V to bring someone back from the dead with her. The kid stood close by her side, holding on to her hand as if he thought she was the one who needed to be afraid. His gaze landed briefly on every face.

At Trent, he stopped. The two of them stared at each other for a long time—too long, I thought. I could feel an odd tension simmering just beneath the surface. Obviously, Trent knew exactly who this guy was. How he felt about him was less clear, for some reason.

Finally, the new kid smiled. I narrowed my eyes, trying to determine what it was that freaked me out about his face, his stance, his whole demeanor. Something about him felt deeply wrong, but I couldn't articulate what, even in my own thoughts.

"It's been a long time, Trent." He had an understated way of speaking, a little too smooth. It didn't quite match his fresh, boyish features. "Good to see you."

"Yeah." Trent made no move to approach. "You too, Dylan." He took an extra few moments to size the kid up. I knew what he was thinking; the same as all of us. *What the fuck is going on here?* But then he seemed to relax enough to offer the kid his hand. They shook. Veronica's smile got bigger.

Logan, Orion, and I said nothing. To my left, I felt the vampire practically boiling in his skin. He hated nothing more than to be left out of the loop, especially when it came to V. And there wasn't much we could do at the moment except watch. Unless, of course, we wanted to attack. But I didn't need to be told how bad an idea that would be.

"Chill," I muttered out of the side of my mouth. "Look how damn happy she is. Let her be."

Orion grimaced. "That's what I don't like," he answered. "I don't trust him."

It was a sentiment widely shared among our motley crew, including Trent the slayer. I'd kind of gotten the impression that he knew Veronica's new friend at least as well as she did, if not better, and yet he didn't look too thrilled to see him walking the earth again. The next time Trent spoke only confirmed my suspicions.

"Don't take this the wrong way," Trent said, "but what are you doing here, dude?"

"I found him." V cut in before the kid called Dylan could reply for himself. "On the other side."

I studied her intently. She was still holding tight to Dylan's hand. Her aura shone huge and bright, but also a little shaky. Was she nervous? I frowned. *Why would she be nervous?* Did she know something we didn't yet?

"Where exactly were you?" Trent's tone was nonchalant, but the gears in his head were turning. He watched Dylan's every move with the intensity of a hawk.

Veronica faltered. "I'm not sure," she admitted. "It was dark and silent, and I saw a lot of people, but no one acknowledged anyone else. Dylan was the only one who could interact with me." She and Dylan looked at each other.

"We found your body here, Veronica," Trent said. Almost at the same time, all of us spectators leaned in to gauge her reaction. Orion was laser-focused on Veronica, like nothing else existed in the world. On the other side of me, Logan stood back impassively. He had gone quiet, but I knew he was absorbing every word.

V's eyes widened slightly. "That's…" She let out her breath. "That's really weird, Trent. I don't know what to say."

Trent continued. "You were dead."

"Yeah, I know." She lifted her chin a bit, the classic sign of defiance brewing in her spirit. "That's what Dylan told me."

"Okay, so you understood what was going on." Trent turned to Dylan. The paper-thin air was now composed entirely of awkwardness.

"I mean, not really." Dylan laughed wryly. "Is this an interrogation, or what? I saw her coming toward me, we talked, and then we found a way out. If that was a one-in-a-million stroke of luck, I won't argue with you. I'll just take it."

"Look, it was either this or we'd be stuck wandering that place for who knows how long? Maybe forever." Veronica squared up to Trent. She was ready to fight if necessary. The hard stubbornness in her expression stirred my blood. I'd always had a soft spot for women who stood their ground. "You don't have to be happy to see us," she said. "But that doesn't change the fact that we're here. And yes, it really is him."

Internally, I winced. I wanted to be in V's corner on this, a hundred percent. I wanted to step up between her and Trent and tell the slayer to fuck off and leave her alone. But the more I saw of this Dylan kid, the more alarms went off in my mind. I still didn't know how to describe the unrest he sparked in me, and that was saying a lot. There wasn't much capable of throwing me off.

But Dylan just set my teeth on edge. I would've liked nothing more than to see the last of him as he tumbled off one of the mountain faces surrounding the peak, and the fact that V was so dead set on defending him pissed me off. I wondered if he might have cast some magic on her, bewitched her somehow.

After a long pause, Trent relented. "All right." He backed up. "You're both fine?"

"Never been better," Dylan answered. Veronica grinned.

"Then let's get out of here." Trent turned.

I couldn't take it anymore. He only got a few feet before I blocked his path. "Absolutely not." I stared into his face. "That guy isn't coming with us."

Trent immediately folded his arms. "I beg your pardon?" he asked wryly.

"Seth..." Veronica's eyes found mine over

Trent's shoulder. "Please don't." Her voice was full of pleading. "Please. I need you to trust me."

I ignored the disturbingly strong urge to back down rather than upset her. She had already been through a lot in the last few hours. But this was a level of apprehension I couldn't put aside. Pointing at Dylan, I said, "He needs to go back to wherever the fuck he came from. Now, preferably."

Dylan's expression shifted from confusion to annoyance tinged with a hint of black anger. I could see something terrible in that subtle undercurrent of rage, something clawing to get out. Like hell I was going to stand by while these idiots brought it back to civilization.

"I'll take this opportunity to remind you, we're not a team," Trent said. "When we get back to Anchorage, you're free to do as you please. All of you. And what that means, is that you have zero say in the decisions I'm making for myself. Dylan's coming home."

I might've bought it if he hadn't hesitated right then. His eyes and his energy betrayed him—he doubted Dylan just as much as I did, if not more. Nonetheless, it was clear that for his own reasons, Trent's mind was made up.

"I trusted you, Seth. Why can't you have any faith in me?" V glared, her pleas replaced by hurt and indignance. "I'm safe. I'm comfortable and back from the dead. Thank you all for helping me, but now I just need some time to catch up with Dylan."

"Back off." Trent brushed past me. "Let's get out of here."

The two slayers and Veronica's mysterious friend went ahead. Orion, Logan, and I tailed them at a fair distance; not enough to lose them on the mountain, but enough to keep healthy space between us and Dylan.

"He's fucked up, right?" I asked the others. "It's not just me?"

Orion shook his head. "I want her away from him," he growled. "As soon as we're back in the city, I'll make sure they're separated. And if that slayer doesn't like it…" He trailed off. I tried not to imagine him and Trent waging war on the lush green lawns of that bourgeoise neighborhood. Normally, the thought would have filled me with chaotic glee. Now it made my stomach turn.

I'd already done a lot to fuck up my connection with V. She was mad, and why not? She thought the hollow-eyed monstrosity she had brought back from the veil was her newest Prince Charming. Until the delusion broke, if it ever did, everything I said made me look like the bad guy.

I hadn't been prepared for her withdrawal to hurt me in any way, much less so deeply. It took every ounce of my limited self-control to keep from snatching her up and trying to fight her head on straight. Until Dylan showed up, I had convinced myself that V was worth all the trouble in the world.

But maybe I was wrong. Despite what I felt for her, which was real and true, the thought of getting wrapped up in this brand-new problem made my skin crawl. I had no desire to find out what was lurking under this new kid's human mask. *That wasn't in the goddamn contract!*

The game had changed, and suddenly, so had my perspective. Things were getting a little too hairy for my liking. I had an inkling that Dylan's presence would only lead to bigger messes. And we were already sort of up to our necks in shit.

I wanted V, badly. In a perfect, simple world, I could have had my cake and eaten it too. But I *didn't* want to mess with anything that wasn't strictly my business—or stay onboard a sinking ship. At the end of the day, I was always gonna look out for number one.

If that meant I had to leave beautiful, strong, fiery V behind—so be it.

At least, that was what I told myself.

CHAPTER 9

ORION

Our excursion to Denali had gone from bad to worse in a remarkably short amount of time. We trudged back down the mountain in a formation that struck me as fundamentally incorrect and unfair. What were the supernaturals doing, following behind slayers like dogs? The further we traveled, the higher my irritation rose.

Never before had I allowed myself to be debased and humiliated in such a way. I could hardly believe it was happening now, except that Veronica's lithe form moved over the inhospitable terrain in front of me, a constant reminder of what I was working toward, of the reward awaiting me at the end of these long trials. I'd already lost close to everything, hadn't I? If swallowing my pride meant I could retain a shred of dignity on which to rebuild, I knew I had no choice.

But the consequences were nearly unbearable. More than anything, I hated to watch Veronica show attraction or affection toward a stranger. How could he have won her over so quickly? Were we really so late? A thousand questions consumed my thoughts, fueled by jealousy, anger, paranoia. A few days ago, I had been so sure that Veronica was mine and no one else's.

Now I battled my way through wind and snow, watching her go ahead arm in arm with another man. The urge to catch up and separate them coursed through my veins like blood, but I had seen how quickly her affection for Seth soured when he spoke his mind. Although the demon's effort was regrettably commendable, I had experienced enough of Veronica's temper to know he'd been foolish. The girl was strong-headed, stubborn as a mule.

And unless I wished to suffer the same kind of spurning, I had no choice but to keep my own mouth shut—at least until we were alone again. Alienating her was something I could not afford at this stage. No matter what else happened, I needed Veronica back. It seemed like that was going to be a challenge with the unwelcome arrival of this boy, but so be it.

Nobody spoke a word during the descent of Denali. We fanned out, each of us seeking our own space. I had no idea what the thoughts of my cohorts were as we came down from the sky, but on the way down toward the foothills where we had left the car, I noticed Logan and Seth both straying farther and farther from the path followed by Veronica and the others.

Where are you going? I asked, reaching out with my mind. *She can't be left alone with them.*

Seth was the first and only one to reply. *You think I'm fucking happy about this? I want to punch that kid's teeth down his throat. But V's stance is pretty clear at the moment, and there's no fucking way I'm gonna get in that damn car with him. We can meet in the city if you want.*

Logan, for his part, said nothing. I glanced in his direction and saw him soaring upward again, wings outspread, quickly becoming little more than a dark silhouette in the distance. He might have looked toward me as he flew off, but it was very hard to tell. Annoyed, I grimaced and shook my head. How far we had fallen in a matter of days. And where the hell was that angel off to, anyway?

"You." Trent's voice caught me off guard. He had stopped just up ahead, waiting for me with Dylan and Veronica behind him. My eyes caught V's for a split second before she looked away, but I'd seen the confusion in her eyes.

I raised an eyebrow to Trent. "What do you want?"

He watched me approach. "You're coming with us. In the car."

I frowned. "Absolutely not. I do not want to do that." The whole scenario struck me as absurdly unfair. Why should the others get to go freely while I was stuck under constant supervision from a mortal man? I longed to assert my rightful dominance over this arrogant human, and yet, Veronica's eyes had returned to me. I could feel her scrutinizing my every action.

"Yeah, well, I'm not giving you a choice," Trent said. "Because you're the one I can't predict."

A dark scowl crossed my face. "I'll take that as a compliment," I muttered.

He smirked. "It wasn't."

Boiling with rage and embarrassment, I submitted to being shepherded the rest of the way off Denali, reminding myself over and over that any amount of humiliation was worth keeping Veronica in my sights at all times. Other than a few passing glances, she seemed determined not to acknowledge me in the presence of her new man, with whom she was clearly infatuated. Something was very wrong here like she'd been brainwashed by him. As soon as the terrain leveled out, their hands linked and were never broken.

By the time we reached the vehicle, only a thin veil of cloud cover shielded me from the sun's rays. Veronica chose to sit with Dylan in the back, thereby relegating me to the front seat. I didn't even complain, my emotions rendered down to a bed of glowing coals. In the rearview mirror, I could see her smiling, gazing with sentimental eyes at the boy she had brought from the other side of the veil.

"Buckle up," Trent said, as the car's engine kicked to life. "It's a little bit of a ride back to Anchorage."

I sank back morosely into my seat. This had already turned into the longest, most arduous journey of my life, and I didn't see that changing anytime soon.

"So you really followed Lian to Alaska, huh?" Dylan grinned. "Man, I always knew you had it bad for her."

"I never made it a secret," Trent replied. His

eyes moved back and forth in the mirror, constantly keeping tabs on everyone.

Dylan laughed. "You played it down. I'm glad she finally got you. Never thought I'd see the day, honestly."

"Good thing we just found out you're the luckiest man in the universe."

In more ways than one, I thought savagely. I hated how badly it stung to know I was replaceable in Veronica's mind and heart. Perhaps the history she shared with this mystery boy gave him something of an unfair edge, but I had always assumed that the connection we had was superior to all others.

"Or," Veronica said, cutting into my thoughts, "we're the lucky ones to have Dylan back." She giggled. My heart hurt. If there was one thing I hadn't missed from my earlier, more romantic days, it was the ache of longing for another. Those feelings had been far in the past for so long. But here they were again, and I lacked the luxury of privacy in order to work through them.

"We'll see about that." Something about Trent's tone caused me to eject from furious introspection to cast a sidelong look at his face. His expression was more or less blank on the surface, but I caught a subtle undercurrent of doubt, of heavy distrust—and not just toward me.

"Oh, come on, Trent. You have to admit this is totally unbelievable." Veronica spoke as if the current turn of events was undeniably a good thing. She sounded as though all her dreams had just come true at once.

"It sure is." Again, Trent's words were laced with the finest strands of doubt and apprehension. His gaze kept flicking over the back seat. Not that Dylan or Veronica noticed; they were much too involved in each other. "It's good to have you back, Dylan."

"It's good to be back, I think." Dylan pressed his finger to the window button and put his hand through the open pane. "I forgot what this all felt like. Hell, I was starting to forget your faces. Everything kind of runs together after a while in that place, you know?" He paused. "But you never forget about the moment of death. That shit stays with you forever."

"I'm sorry," Veronica said softly. "I wish I had done more save you. I would've done everything in my power…" She trailed off. I hoped she wouldn't speak anymore.

"It's not your fault. None of this is your fault."

I closed my own eyes and focused all my energy

on a plan to separate them. There was only so much of this shallow nonsense I could take. Couldn't she tell that something was seriously wrong with him? Maybe with her too.

Of course, she couldn't. I didn't want to admit the truth, but Veronica had clearly been in love with this boy at some previous moment in time. Her judgment, normally sharp for a mortal, was being clouded by the passion that I admired so much when it was directed at me. Even if she knew he wasn't right on the inside, I wondered if she would care.

"I'm just glad you're here," she said.

"We're going to see her, right?" V asked. Her voice brightened further at the mention of her friend. "Like, you're taking us back to her house?"

Trent was quiet for a minute. "I'm not sure that would be the best idea," he said at last. "Not right now. She's been through a lot already over the last few days. I don't know how to explain this to her yet."

"Oh." Disappointment colored Veronica's tone. She recovered fast. "In that case, I'd like to formally request that you drop us off at the Grand Hotel."

My hackles went up. I sat up in the seat, suddenly tense. My jaw clenched as I waited for Trent's response. If he gave the wrong one, I'd handle things myself, restraint be damned. I refused to allow her to spend any time on her own with Dylan. None at all.

"Who's *us*?" Trent shot me a warning glance; he had seen my visceral reaction. I drove a hand into my hair, holding it there. All of my self-control had become abruptly dedicated to not jumping straight for Dylan's throat. The mere implication of Veronica being with him was almost more than I could handle.

"Dylan and me," she said innocently. "I thought he could stay with me at the hotel. It'd give you and Lian a break from hosting."

Trent laughed. "No. That is not happening."

"Dude, you sound like my dad," Dylan remarked. "When I was like fifteen. What's the big deal?"

"Seriously?" Trent's smile faded. "Both of you have endured some serious supernatural shit very recently. We have no idea what kind of trauma could be associated with dying, hanging out in an unknown purgatory space, and then bringing two spirits back into the realm of the living. You need to be under some kind of supervision for a while until we know that everything is really okay." He looked at Dylan. "Come on. You know how this works."

"Yeah, yeah. I was just playing." Dylan turned his face to the window.

"Then what are we going to do? We're not going to see Lian, so…" Veronica was irritated that her plans had been foiled. She chewed her lower lip.

I saw my chance and took it. "Veronica can come with me. Only Veronica."

"Normally, I'd say no," Trent said. "But this time, I don't think I can. As long as Logan will be there too, you guys can keep an eye on her."

"Yes," I grumbled. The mortals always adored Logan, for reasons I didn't fully understand.

"Excuse me! I don't need to be babysat, Trent." Veronica leaned forward.

"It's not babysitting," he said. "We're taking care of you, all right? Lian would lose her mind if she found out I let you go off on your own after you literally died on a mountain. Once we know it's all fine, you can go back to doing whatever you want."

She sighed. "You're right. Sorry."

"Thank you. Dylan and I will find a place to crash for tonight. I'll tell Lian we'll see her later, and we will figure this out in the meantime."

"Okay." She lapsed into silence without saying anything to me. I was annoyed at her, but still grateful that she was not going to be away from me any longer.

"Where are we going?" Trent asked me. "I'll drop you and V off first." I gave him the address of the house by the inlet, and he nodded. Then he looked at me—face to face, not in the rearview mirror. "If I catch you doing anything shady, and I mean anything, I know where to find you now."

"Ugh, Trent…" Veronica buried her face in her hands. "Can you just drive there, please?"

"You have my word." I had to pull the sentence out of my mouth one word at a time as if they were teeth. But I said it, and he seemed to accept the promise.

"Fine," he said. "Let's go."

Dylan looked at me and gave me that half-smile again, the one that made my heart go a million miles an hour. A smile I swore I'd never see again, and right now it felt like I've been given a chance to make up for the not saving him. Nothing seemed to matter now that I knew my time in Anchorage was all leading up to being able to see him, hear him, touch him.

Though I wouldn't lie that my feelings for Orion, Seth, and Logan hadn't changed. They'd just become complicated now with Dylan back.

"How's it feel to be back among the living?" I said quietly.

"I should ask you the same thing," he replied. Then he thought about it for a moment. "Honestly? It's pretty weird. Turns out you can get used to just about anything—even death. But I'm not complaining." He squeezed my fingers in his.

A rush of warmth surged through my body. "Neither am I." Actually, that wasn't quite true. I resented Trent and Orion's decision to keep us apart. *Of course, this is the one thing they come to an agreement on.* At the same time, I knew better than to rock the boat too much right away. We all needed time to get acclimated.

Soon Trent would see that Dylan hadn't changed a bit. He was the same loving, funny guy we'd always known. Sure, he'd been through hell and back, maybe literally, but at that point, so had we all. The strength of Dylan's spirit was reflected in the fact that he had come out on the other side unscathed.

Has he?

The thought burst into my mind with the force of a grenade, and to my immense chagrin, I couldn't make it go away. It was so hard to admit that anything could be wrong while he was right there in front of me, his chest rising and falling with every corporeal breath. And yet, there was the faintest trill of foreboding in the back of my head. This all seemed way too good to be true. That I was forgetting something. And maybe it was too good to be true.

All of a sudden, I had all the luck in the world. But I'd never been an especially lucky person. Particularly as far as Dylan was concerned.

"Uh, V?" He waved his hand gently over my face. "You're staring."

"Oh, sorry." I laughed and tried to convince myself that it was just the old paranoia rearing its head, and that I was being ridiculous. "It's so crazy. One minute I thought you were gone forever, and the next, here you are."

"Yeah," he said. "Here I am."

Trent just drove until the car pulled up the long driveway leading to Orion's house. Then he killed the engine and caught my eye, a stare whose meaning I understood immediately. *Get the hell out.*

"All right, all right. Fine. Even though I don't have any stuff with me, and I haven't eaten in like, a day and a half."

"Don't worry about it, V," Dylan told me soothingly. "I'll see you soon." He lifted his hand and touched the tips of his fingers to my cheek.

"Bye."

"Let's go." Orion spoke sternly. He punctuated the command by slamming the car door. I rolled my eyes, but left without a choice, and followed him up to the old porch stairs. Behind me, I heard Trent start up the engine again and pull the car out. I glanced over my shoulder. All I saw was Trent in the driver's seat, plus an outline of Dylan sitting in the back.

"That's weird," I muttered under my breath.

"What?" Orion pushed the door open. He stalked across the threshold, turned around, and glared at me.

"Nothing." I held up my hands in mock surrender. "Dylan and Trent used to be best friends. I figured he would want to sit up front after we got out. That's all." Orion eyed me up and down, plainly disbelieving of every word I said. I took a deep breath and let it go. "Thank you for coming after me, and sorry I was so distracted by Dylan. It's just that I never expected to see him again after he died... after I didn't save him. Anyway, you didn't have to come for me, but thanks."

"Yes, we did." He moved toward me abruptly, as if he was going to grab me by the shoulders, but at the last moment, his demeanor changed. I found myself wrapped in a tight embrace, possessive, but not unkind. "Don't act tough, Veronica. You needed us." Orion paused. "Both of you."

There was something so damn intoxicating about being in his arms. I closed my eyes and gave up resistance, leaning deep into his chest. His fingers ran through my hair, and I felt a twinge of guilt. Dylan and I had only just reunited, yet I could not stay away from my tall, dark vampire. There was no denying what I felt for him, but my mind felt twisted and so distracted by Dylan's return. I never realized how much guilt I held onto until I saw him again. How I wanted madly to make him understand that I wanted to save him. I hadn't worked out how I would deal with the old emotions awakening inside me for Dylan. Especially when recently, I'd found myself falling for three others… a vampire, a demon, and a fallen angel.

Nonetheless, Dylan stayed impossible to forget. His face drifted in the darkness behind my eyelids. I loved knowing that he was in a car at this very moment, heading to a hotel to spend a night catching up with Trent. But it was haunting too, in a way I couldn't hope to articulate.

"How are you feeling?" Orion finally inquired, a little brusquely. He led me from the front hall into the living room, which was empty and still. I looked around, ears open for any other signs of life.

"I think I'm fine." We talked casually, like I hadn't died and been resurrected hours earlier. "Where are Logan and Seth?"

He scowled. "I don't know. I can only assume

they'll show up eventually. You should eat." Before I could protest, or even say anything else, a loud growl from my stomach answered for me. Orion promptly left my side for the first time since we exited the car and disappeared into the kitchen.

A few moments later, I followed. The energy between us was undeniably different, and I felt surprisingly bad about that. Alone with Orion, it was quickly apparent that whatever my feelings for Dylan were, they did not erase those I already had. My empty stomach twisted into a knot. The silence turned deafening.

"So…what do you think?" I leaned in the door-way, pretending I wasn't scared shitless of his answer. I had no idea what to do if he forced me to choose—between him, Dylan, Logan, or Seth. The longer I dwelled on it, the more I realized I might be totally screwed.

Nice fucking job, V. Getting entangled with four guys who hate each other's guts. I rubbed a hand across my face. No way this was going to end well.

Orion stopped. He was standing at the counter, and I could see him processing the question. Then he turned and tossed me an apple. "You don't really want to know," was what he said. "Trust me."

I caught the fruit and checked it over. Past experiences had taught me that immortal beings weren't always great at knowing about human staples such as expiration dates or over-ripeness. "No, I do," I said.

"You don't," Orion repeated. He guided me back to the living room sofa. "It will upset you."

"And?" I bit into the apple and almost collapsed under the sudden weight of its deliciousness. The sweet juice flooded my starved tastebuds. I sort of moaned through a mouthful of fruit. "Don't you like to argue?"

Orion actually chuckled. "Not while you're enjoying yourself so much. We will have time to argue in the future."

I took another bite. "I hate the sound of that. Would it kill you to stop being so damn cryptic and just speak your mind? I'm literally asking for it." It wasn't like him not to be offensively forthcoming with his opinions. I wondered what had happened during my little spiritual excursion. "Seriously. I won't be mad."

Orion sat on the sofa with his arm around me, full of thoughts but voicing none of them. Once I devoured the apple, his unresponsiveness began to grate. The moment I opened my mouth to press him, however, he said, "Are you in love with him?"

I blinked. "Is that somehow a trick question?" I

had the distinct suspicion that he was trying to lure me into dangerous territory.

"Yes," he admitted. "I already know the answer."

"I…" I hesitated, which made me feel awful. "I was. Back in Seattle."

Orion's eyes narrowed slightly. "Not now, on Denali? Or in the Underworld, as you wandered together?"

The familiar note of challenge in his voice made me bristle. "We were in there for like five minutes. At least, that's what it seemed like. And…I guess I don't know how to answer that. I see him, and I feel the way I felt that last time, so many years ago. Maybe that is love."

He grimaced. "Or a shadow of it. A shell."

I frowned. "Jealousy doesn't look good on you."

"I'm not jealous," he lied. "You need to be careful, Veronica. Death affects everyone in strange ways, mortals most of all. You think you know whom you brought back to this realm, but do you?"

His ongoing questions wouldn't have bothered me so much if I had been a hundred percent sure of my own convictions. I knew that, and it made me mad. It made me want to take his arm from around my shoulders and put some distance between us on the couch. In the background, the seedling of skepticism I kept trying to kill threatened to take root.

"I think I'd know better than you," I retorted, fully aware of how my promise to not get mad inched closer and closer to breaking. "Dylan and I were tight, whether you like it or not. I know his heart."

I expected Orion's temper to flare at any moment. We were like a gas can and a match when we argued; it was only a matter of time before it blew up in our faces. This time, however, he simply regarded me with a strange, inscrutable expression on his maddeningly handsome face. Despite my brewing anger, I realized how much I'd missed him, and how thankful I was that he and the boys had come for me.

He leaned over and pressed his lips to my forehead. They were cool, in a familiar, comforting sort of way. "I've been there before," he said quietly. "Where you are. For your sake, I want you to be right. But I know that you are wrong."

"Well, you're not helping." I folded my arms.

"There's no way for me to help, even though I want to," he answered. I detected a weird hint of melancholy in his voice, one I had never heard previously. Not to mention the fact that this was the first time he had ever expressed a desire to help with anything.

"Yeah, there is." I nudged his shoulder. "You could order me some more food." It was easier to focus on resolving the ongoing problem of my hunger, instead of the tiny cracks already appearing in my new, deceptively perfect reality.

CHAPTER 11

SETH

Logan and I separated pretty fast on our way back to the city. One minute he was there in the sky, and the next, he was gone. I didn't think too much of it; if he had taught me anything, it was that fallen angels were some of the ficklest beings in the known universe. It was impossible to understand where he was or what he was doing, so I just shrugged and let it roll off my back. He'd turn up eventually.

Without him, I rolled up to Orion's house alone, having beaten the car by what I assumed to be a pretty wide margin. The fact that Logan was nowhere to be seen didn't surprise me at all—he wouldn't have bailed if not for his own secret purpose. But the solitude was a good thing as far as I was concerned. The moment I stepped through the door, fatigue hit me like a brick wall. I almost stumbled on my way up the stairs.

"Goddamn," I muttered. "Where the hell is this coming from?" Exhaustion wasn't an experience I was used to, nor did I appreciate it. But all of a sudden, I felt like I'd been run over by a truck from Hell. "All right, fuck it." I made my way to my room, yawning so wide my jaw crackled. "I guess it's time for a nap."

When was the last time I had taken one of those? But as soon as my head hit the pillow, I was out—for a minute.

At first, when I opened my eyes again, a sickening sense of familiarity punched me in the gut. The cold got to me first, dancing across my skin like a hundred tiny needles. "Ah, shit." I sat up, rubbing my face. "You've gotta be fucking kidding me." I glanced around at shadow-cloaked walls and wondered if I'd actually been asleep the whole time and was just now waking up for real. "If this is a joke, it's not funny."

My call received no response. Then I blinked, and everything disappeared. The walls, the floor, even the cold, all gone. I found myself floating in the midst of the deepest black void I'd ever seen. Everywhere I turned was dark emptiness.

"Okay." I took a deep breath. "Maybe it's not a joke."

It was hard to move through the nothingness, as if the air below my knees was made of something thick and viscous. I picked a random direction and started trudging. "If I ever find out who's behind this bullshit, I'm gonna fucking kill them." I stopped for a moment, glanced over my shoulder, then realized there was no way to measure how far I had gone. "Good. Great."

Then I faced forward and saw someone in the distance, just standing there. I should have been thrilled to find company for my misery, but the sight of that figure sent a prickle of foreboding up the back of my neck. Still, I kept moving closer; I'd already spent weeks working with a couple of assholes I didn't like. One more wasn't going to kill me.

At least, I hoped not.

"Hey," I shouted across the darkness. The figure remained motionless, staring blankly in my direction. "Can you—"

I stopped. The realization had just dawned on me that I recognized that face, and that there was something wrong with it. Veronica's creepy little boyfriend didn't look any better with blacked-out eyes. He opened his mouth to speak, and a trail of dark smoke leaked out.

"Oh, no." I shook my head. "No. Nope. Fuck this." As if on cue, the invisible floor fell out from under my feet, and I plummeted down into the belly of the void.

Next thing I knew, I was sitting bolt upright in my bed at Orion's house, catching my breath. I swore the temperature in the room had dropped by at least ten degrees. My suspicions had been pretty strong to begin with, but now I was dead certain. There was something horribly wrong with that kid.

"Fuck." I got out of the bed. "He's gonna fucking kill her."

The stairs creaked like mad on my way up to the vampire's room. If he was in there, he heard me coming a mile away, and I didn't even care. On this particular playing field, Orion and I were equals, or as close as we could possibly get. For once, I was reasonably sure he'd understand exactly where I was coming from.

His door was cracked a little bit, but I still knocked. The look on his face when he saw it was me standing in the hall would have been a hundred times more satisfying if I hadn't resolved to be his civil ally for the time being.

"Seth." He frowned. "What is it? You look like shit."

"Yeah? I suppose you're speaking from experience," I retorted. A brief, wry grin flashed across his face. "Sorry." I sighed. "Look, can I talk to you about that guy V dragged in from the Underworld, or wherever the fuck she was?"

Orion's gaze and posture sharpened instantly. He stepped back from the door, motioning me inside. The door closed behind me. "What do you know?" he asked.

"Nothing!" I threw my hands up. "Not a goddamned thing, but I can take some guesses. And you know what? They're all bad!" I told him about the dream from which I had just woken. "That son of a bitch isn't human. I don't know *what* he is. But I think he's a danger to her, and I think he's got an agenda." Driven by anger, my voice began to rise.

Orion gestured for me to be quiet. "Be calm. She's here."

"What?" I shot a reflexive glance toward the closed door. "V? Where?"

"Down in the den." Orion grimaced. "She's angry. She wants to be alone."

"He isn't here too, is he?" I half-whispered.

"Of course not. That's why she's upset." He

paused. "The other slayer would not allow them to remain together either. A rare show of mutual agreement." It seemed painful for him to admit he shared anything in common with a slayer, especially viewpoints.

"Okay. So we agree, he's fucked," I said. "I just don't know how, or why. And I don't believe for a fucking second that she just happened to find him out there on the other side of the veil. Someone made sure he was in the right place at the right time." I looked Orion in the eyes. "He's a puppet. He has to be."

I expected him to tell me flat-out that I was wrong, an idiot, and I hadn't thought things through. But this time, Orion simply nodded.

"I agree," he admitted. "Unfortunately, I don't have any more answers than you." He glanced away. "I'm at a disadvantage when it comes to matters beyond the mortal realm. However, we both know someone who isn't."

I had never heard Orion acknowledge any kind of deficiency whatsoever, and if we hadn't been in the midst of such a heavy discussion, I might have asked him to repeat himself. As it was, I had to take his unexpected candor at face value and nod back.

"Logan," I said. "Let's go get him."

That turned out to be easier said than done.

Logan's door stood uncharacteristically open, his room empty. The window on the far wall was also ajar, curtains billowing in a light breeze. I could see the sun just beginning its descent toward midafternoon.

Orion folded his arms. "He always does this."

I ran a hand through my hair. "We should have known."

CHAPTER 12

LOGAN

I hovered in the sky above the inlet, wings beating the air just enough to keep me high aloft. Shiny beads of sunlight reflected off the water. I closed my eyes, focused my mind, and conjured up the grotesque face of the wendigo. Ever since the arrival of Veronica's companion, I hadn't been able to keep the wendigo out of my thoughts. I couldn't explain exactly why, but questions about the creature consumed me.

Where had it gone? Why didn't it return? I knew better than anyone that the monster's condition was far too healthy for it to have died or disappeared completely. If it was banished somehow, I would've felt it. We should have seen some evidence of its ghastly existence near Veronica's body on the mountaintop. But the site had been clean; no blood, no footprints, no unduly disturbed snow. I had pressing questions, and in search of answers, I'd decided to go straight to the source.

The summons rang out loud and clear, resonating along the threads of energy that bound the mortal plane. There was no way the creature couldn't hear it if it was able. Now all I had to do was wait for a response. And initially, I received none. Turning in a slow circle, I scanned the horizon all around, searching for signs of a wendigo speeding toward my location.

Nothing. The half-wild Alaskan landscape rolled away in all directions, unchanged.

But then I caught the faintest glimmer of an echo coming from a place much nearer than I had expected. I kept turning, waiting for that tiny signal to sound off right in front of me. When it finally did, I looked down and furrowed my brow.

I was facing the house, so close I could see the window I'd left open in my room. The echo came from beyond, but not far. In the distance, I saw the outline of downtown, and I knew.

The wendigo's energy was there.

I returned to my room to find Seth and Orion standing in the doorway. They both looked at me expectantly. I folded my wings and shut the window.

Then I said, "The wendigo came back to the city. I don't know what's going on."

"Neither do we," Orion answered. "But we don't like it."

Seth stared at me. "You're sure that thing is here somewhere?"

"Yeah. It can't be far. If I call out, I can feel it." As a matter of fact, I still could, an almost magnetic pull drawing me toward the city. "I think it has something to do with the boy."

The expressions on their faces told me I didn't need to elaborate any further. The demon turned toward the hallway. "Can you take us there?"

I started to say yes, but Orion stopped me. "No." He gave Seth a meaningful glance. "Veronica can't be left alone. For now, we stay here. She's our priority."

Seth didn't like it, but he conceded. "Fine. For now." He shifted his weight impatiently. "Maybe if we all go, she'll talk to us."

Orion chuckled grimly. "I doubt it." He was quiet for a moment. "But it's worth a shot. Come on."

Together, we went down the stairs to the first-floor den. Veronica was curled up on the sofa, gripping a mug with both hands and staring out at a bright view that contrasted her gloomy expression. Her frown only deepened once she realized we were all there, watching her.

"Look who's here," she muttered unhappily. "What do you guys want?"

CHAPTER 13

VERONICA

*E*ven though I was pissed at being stonewalled from spending time alone with Dylan, it was still exciting to see the trio come into the den and gather around me on the couch. I kept any visible emotion to a bare minimum, unwilling to give them the satisfaction. I wanted to keep believing they were the bad guys in this scenario; it made me feel better about the creeping doubts that still hadn't gone away.

"Just checking on you," Orion said mildly, as if he had no clue why I might be angry. "Seeing how you are."

"I'm fine. Feel free to leave me alone." Instead of bristling at the rejection, Orion leaned back against the couch cushions.

"No, I don't think we will," he said matter-of-factly. "Actually, I think we'll all sleep down here tonight. Just in case."

"Ugh." I picked up a nearby pillow and threw it at him. "What is wrong with you? Dylan isn't dangerous. He'd never hurt me. I'm sorry you're jealous, but I don't know what else to tell you." I hated the way those words sounded to my own ears as they rolled off my tongue. Like I was lying or covering for someone who was. Why was it so hard to get rid of the whispers of paranoia in the back of my head?

But I knew that if all three of the trio were concerned, there must be a problem. Orion had been overprotective literally from the moment I met him. And Seth could be too reactive, a hothead who acted before he thought. Logan, though? He was an oasis of serenity in the middle of a passionate maelstrom. I'd never seen him do, say, or think anything he didn't wholeheartedly mean.

And there he was, just as concerned as the others. In a way, it was sweet—not to mention surreal to see them pulling together for my sake. I inched further into the corner of the sofa to give them a little more room.

"Seriously, I'm good," I said, fully aware that any of my excuses were falling on deaf ears. "I just need some time to decompress and process everything that's been happening. 'Cause, you know… it's kind of a lot."

"Go ahead." Orion wasn't bothered in the slightest. "We promise not to disturb you."

"That's right," Seth added quickly. "Some of us are very good at brooding in silence." His gaze ricocheted between Orion and Logan.

I laughed before I could help myself. "Oh my God, stop it. Get the hell out of here." I pushed lamely on Orion's shoulder. He didn't budge. "You guys don't need to babysit me. I'm a big girl. I can take care of myself."

"That might not be the best thing to say when you're fresh off a kidnapping that resulted in your death." Seth was not impressed by my reasoning.

I rolled my eyes. "Okay, but I did come back."

"Logan brought you back," Orion pointed out.

I looked to Logan for some kind of help. He shrugged. Then he reached over Orion and brushed a loose strand of hair out of my face. Despite my annoyance, I melted a little. The fact that they still had such an effect on me—all of them—was frustrating and exciting at the same time.

"Thanks for that," I said glumly. "I guess I should be nicer to you, considering the circumstances. I just—" I heaved a huge sigh and let my hands fall to my sides. "Do you understand what it feels like to see a person you thought was gone forever, right in front of you like that?" Vulnerability was not part of my plan, but once I started talking about it, the words poured out. "I can't help but be drawn to him. It's like unfinished business, like there's so much I want him to understand. To see if he really forgives me."

Seth was biting his tongue, hard. I could tell by the way he watched me in silence, his lips carefully locked shut. He held out longer than I thought he would, but eventually, his patience and willpower expired. "You don't feel it?" he asked, exasperated.

"What?" I arched my eyebrows, challenging him. If he had shit to talk about Dylan, I wanted to hear it out loud.

"He's not right, Veronica." Seth's tone softened. "I'm not being a dick this time."

My conscience begged me to back down and agree with him, to embrace my own persistent misgivings. But the part of me that still loved Dylan and had grieved him every single day in the years since his death refused to let him be dragged through the mud.

"You don't know him like I do," I said defensively. "Just because he was a slayer doesn't mean you get to automatically assume the worst. I think

I deserve the opportunity to catch up with him again."

"He was a slayer?" For a moment, I thought I saw worry flash across Logan's icy blue eyes. It passed as quickly as it might have arrived, and I tried to brush it off.

"Yeah, in Seattle. Years ago." I flicked my hair. I glanced out the window. "After Dylan died, Lian tried to help me heal. I'm not sure how well it worked."

"What exactly was it that you lost?" Orion kept his tone neutral. He talked slowly, choosing each word with care. I knew that he was trying very hard not to come off too harsh, though it must have pained him to hear me speak of another man the way I spoke about Dylan.

I decided not to pull any punches. "Everything." Reaching over, I took his hand. "You don't want to hear this, and I apologize for that. But I thought he was my soul mate. My other half. I expected us to grow old and die together."

"That didn't happen," Logan murmured.

"No." A lump threatened to form in my throat. "It didn't. Dylan died in a horrible, brutal way, and I never got any kind of closure. I just had to go on with life as if nothing happened." I swallowed hard, willing the tears not to come. "You know how fast people forget you when you die? Really fast." I let out my breath. "Really fucking fast."

They didn't say anything. I looked at their faces, and only Logan gazed directly back.

"It's true," he said quietly. "Mortal memory is cruel and limited."

"I had to honor him," I continued. "Somehow, in some way. I wanted him to know, wherever he was, that he hadn't been completely erased. So I became a slayer like he was, except I wanted to forge my own path. I figured staying independent would keep me from meeting the same fate as he did." I laughed without humor. "It's worked pretty well so far."

"Let me ask you something." Seth blew a ring of smoke that drifted lazily up toward the ceiling. The sun reflected off his golden eyes, making them ethereal and vibrant. "What would you do if it turned out this man wasn't the person you thought he was?"

"What do you mean?" I attempted to keep the dread out of my voice.

"What if he didn't have the same soul?" Seth was calm as the surface of a still lake. "Or any soul at all. What if you found out he was hollow inside?"

"I don't know," I answered honestly. My voice wavered on the last word.

"That's enough." Orion sat up. He slipped his arm around my shoulders and drew me close. "All we want is to keep you safe, my love. There are many dangers lurking in the dark, and until we know for sure that you won't be harmed, we're going to keep you in our sight." He kissed my forehead.

Emotionally spent, I gave up and leaned into him. But his love and strength did not reassure me this time. I had an awful, creeping suspicion that we were all hurtling as one toward a point of no return.

CHAPTER 14

ORION

I wasn't used to seeing Veronica in distress. Although I deeply resented Dylan's sudden, unwelcome presence in her life, it pained me to know that I had caused her grief. My reluctance to share her didn't mean a blatant disregard for her happiness. By the time night was beginning to fall, she'd settled down somewhat, but tension still lingered.

Late in the evening, Seth tapped me on the shoulder. "You get first watch," he said, arching an eyebrow.

"Can you all just relax?" Veronica cut in before I had a chance to reply. "Nothing is going to happen." She gave me a look that was equal parts fatigue and exasperation. "Wherever Dylan is right now, Trent's there too. He won't be letting Dylan out of his sight." She sighed. "Trust me."

"Consider it a precaution," I told her. "If he doesn't show up tonight, that's great. If he does, we'll be ready." She rolled her eyes but didn't protest any further. Seth, Logan, and I glanced at each other. "I've got this. See you in the morning." They nodded. I knew they would have preferred to stay with her, especially Seth, and I wondered briefly about the motive behind this uncharacteristic show of deference, courtesy, or whatever he might have called it.

"Night, V," he said as he left. "Sleep tight." Logan smiled at her and followed in his wake.

She waved as they left the room, and then she turned to me. "What, you didn't want all four of us sharing a room? I'm shocked."

"This wasn't my idea," I said. Which was true, but I couldn't deny that these new, intimate circumstances pleased me. It seemed like eternity since I'd been alone with her. I almost felt like an entirely different person.

Veronica narrowed her eyes. "Not sure I believe that. Everything is your idea around here."

I chuckled flatly. "Well, it used to be." We were silent for a moment, during which she studied my face with her raptly attentive eyes. I sensed her scrutinizing my face; what was she looking for? An ulterior motive? Traces of a lie? Little did she know that despite however she chose to interpret my intentions, I had practically nothing to deceive her over anymore. Yes, I still desired to turn her, but the new developments of the past few days, plus the rapid shift in dynamic between myself, the angel, and the demon had thrown a large wrench into my plans.

For now, everything I had so carefully designed was pushed aside—not forgotten, but unavoidably delayed. I needed my place of power back, and I needed to know that I had the support of a strong and willing clan.

"Is this about what happened in the grove?" Veronica said abruptly. A hint of compassion softened the bluntness of her tone. "Things are bad now, aren't they?"

I half-grinned at her. "That's awfully presumptuous of you, my darling. You could hurt my feelings if you aren't careful."

"I'm serious." She picked my hand up off her shoulder. "Don't take this the wrong way, Orion, but you don't feel the same. And..." She hesitated. "I could kind of tell that things have changed with the others too."

"Hmm." I glanced away. "I didn't know you were so perceptive."

Veronica shrugged. "Me neither." She ran the slender fingers of her other hand through her thick hair. I caught a mild draft of her scent, just enough to excite my spirit. How I still longed to possess her as my own! She was made to be my thrall. "But I can tell. And I don't necessarily think it's bad, to be honest."

"Why would you?" I frowned. "You're not the one who narrowly avoided losing everything in that forest." The gravity of the clan's situation hadn't struck me hard until that instant, as I sat on the old sofa in the den with Veronica nestled up against my side. My hand, holding hers, reflexively attempted to curl into a fist. She squeezed back.

"No, not this time. But I've been there." She gazed up at me. "And I *did* die today, so…"

"Okay. I'll give you that one." Her face, gentled by empathy, seemed to glow so close to mine, perfect features mapping out the shape of true beauty. I forgot everything, just looking at her. The next thing I knew, our lips had met.

She let me kiss her for a long time, until my starved appetite had been whetted by her touch, her taste. "You know," she whispered, after we finally eased apart, "this is really pushing your luck."

I kissed her again, drawing a delicate moan from the tip of her tongue. "If you don't want to be with me, say so now."

A beat passed. I felt her thinking. Then her hands crept underneath my shirt. She flattened her palms on my skin.

"I'm not going to do that." One swift, fluid movement pushed the shirt over my head, and her mouth found my neck and chest. The warmth of her skin burned mine as we shed our layers one by one. I could barely recall the last time I'd regarded anybody with such reverence, let alone a mortal one.

"How can you be so beautiful?" I murmured into the curve of her hip. My fingers had made their way between her thighs, to the soft valley where her pleasure was made.

Veronica shuddered. "Does it make you mad?" She watched me, chewing her lip, one hand tangled carelessly in her wild mane of hair. She wriggled out of her jeans and pants swiftly, pushing the clothes to the floor with her leg.

I stroked her clit. Her eyes closed. She made a low, guttural sound that rose from a deep, primal place in her chest. "Don't you understand that you are fragile? Temporary?" I traced the same path with my tongue. She was so wet and tasted delicious. "It is a truth that ought to haunt you."

Veronica arched her back. "Oh my God, shut up." She placed her hand on the back of my head, urging me to taste her deeper. "I thought you were going someplace sexy with that. We can talk about your existential philosophy later."

I obliged her request passionately. It was frighteningly easy to lose myself in her and go to a place where nothing except the frenzied entwining of our bodies existed. She grabbed at me, braced herself on the sofa, and let her head fall back. I saw her lips move occasionally when I came up for air, but her sounds were beyond words.

Every muscle in Veronica's lean, taut body tensed at the moment of climax. She cried out, perhaps louder than she meant to. Her fingers dug into my skin, and into the worn leather of the couch. A fine sheen of sweat made her glisten in the dim light as her body shuddered and her thighs clasped tightly around my head.

"Holy fuck, you are amazing." She relaxed, catching her breath. Her heart thrummed in her chest, the blood racing through her veins.

I could turn her now, I thought. *While she's vulnerable and her guard is down.* A month ago, I might have pounced on her without hesitation. Instead, I wrapped her in my arms. The drive to make her mine remained, but it no longer carried a hard, brutal edge. I didn't want to hurt Veronica. Maybe I didn't even want to own her. I wanted to love her.

"I missed you." She pushed her hair away from her face and sat up enough to kiss me fiercely. "Don't tell Dylan."

I caught her chin in my hand. "Tell me honestly. Can he give you this?"

"I don't know." She climbed on top and took me in her hands.

I would've replied, but a blinding flash of pleasure stopped me. I stared up at her, robbed of speech. "You and I are here, and that's all I care about."

Using her mouth and tongue, she sucked down on my cock. She brought me to the very edge of ecstasy, dancing along that fine line. She teased me until it ached sweetly, and then she lay back on the couch, spreading those gorgeous legs for me. Her inner thighs and pussy glistened from her arousal, and that only had my erection hardening. I took over from there; my appetite would no longer be denied. A few ravenous minutes later, and I leaned over her, pushing inside of her. She was tight, and her back arched, her body so responsive to me. I adored everything about her. One hand on the cushion, and the other on the back of the couch, I pumped into her, while she curled her legs around my hips, riding me. Her moans were addictive, and a vampire could easily fall deeper for a slayer as beautiful as V. It wasn't long before she screamed her second climax into a pillow, and we collapsed together.

"We both needed that," she said after a while. "Badly."

"Yes," I agreed. "And I could go again and again."

She rolled over and kissed me, laughing. A mischievous spark lit up her tender gaze. "Do you think they heard us?"

I stole another kiss. "It doesn't matter. They definitely know."

Veronica giggled. "Are you going to fight about it later?" She was tugging a little bit on my emotions, trying to get a rise out of me. I had no doubt about it, and for once I didn't care. The fact that we had all managed to unite for a single cause had changed my perspective by the tiniest bit, washed away some of the bitter jealousy.

"Do you want that?" I asked, amused. "I'm sure it wouldn't be hard to get Seth to throw a punch."

"No." She rested her head on my chest. "But it's nice to be desired."

Before long, her breathing had slowed into the pattern of sleep. A sharp, irrational thought intruded upon my consciousness: that I'd better keep an eye on her to ensure she didn't slip right back into the no-man's-land behind the veil. I kept one hand in the middle of her naked back, counting each rise and fall. Through the night that was how I kept time, too paranoid to sleep.

Veronica was alive, and she was precious. Holding her was like holding a cosmic treasure against my body, feeling its rhythm and trying to fall in sync. If I closed my eyes too, I could almost see my purpose realigning. I wanted her to be the only thing that mattered.

And yet, there were shadows accruing on the horizon. The state of his clan, the missing wendigo, the distant knowledge that far away in Seattle, plans for war were likely brewing. I could not afford to lose my focus.

But for the shortest of moments, I indulged in Veronica's love. She slept in my arms.

I waited for sunrise.

We walked half a mile into Bootlegger's Cove, to a café for breakfast with Veronica. The counter in the front was busy, the air thick with the scent of coffee. Veronica spent a while studying the menu board while we sort of hung around behind her and tried to look inconspicuous.

"Hey, are you guys being served?" The friendly young man behind the counter grinned at us. "The counter's pretty full, but feel free to take a booth if you'd like. Someone should be over soon to get your order."

"Anywhere?" Seth asked. He was making a real effort to act human and pretend he cared about things like manners, with varying degrees of success. His discomfort was palpable, but I had to give credit where credit was due; so far, he'd managed not to twist any heads off or scorch an innocent business establishment down to the foundation.

The guy nodded, making a welcoming gesture with his arm. "Anywhere you want. We'll be right with you."

Seth glanced at us. Veronica laughed. "What are you waiting for?" she teased. "You heard him. Pick a booth." As he awkwardly carved a path through the bustling diner floor, Veronica took Orion and me by one hand each and pulled us along in his wake. "This feels like a fucked-up sitcom," she remarked, her voice cheerful. "I don't think I hate it."

To no one's surprise, Seth beelined for a booth in the farthest possible corner of the restaurant. But then, Orion surprised everyone by backing off and letting me slide in next to Veronica. He wasn't thrilled about it, but there was a grudging acknowledgement of obligation in the way he said, "It's your turn." She looked between us, holding her breath, waiting for the tension to break.

I said, "Thanks" and reached for a menu.

"Wow," Veronica whispered under her breath. She turned for a moment to Seth, who shrugged. "Okay. I'm not going to pretend I understand why you're all suddenly playing nice, but you won't hear me complaining either." She leaned over, resting her cheek on my shoulder so that she could peer at the same menu. "Do you guys have pancakes in Hell or wherever? If not, you should definitely try some." She kissed my shoulder. "With syrup."

"Yeah?" I didn't know how to explain to her that my senses hadn't been the same for ages. I could eat, but food tasted like dust in my mouth, and the smells were more like memories of scent. Part of the atonement for my sins was a life dimmed of the joy that had been thrown away in my first life.

"I just realized I've literally never seen any of you eat anything. Except for Seth, but that's mostly alcohol."

The demon grinned. "So what? It's the only thing you got here that's worth ingesting. And by the way, it's not just 'Hell or wherever.' You've been there now; you ought to start learning what to call it."

Veronica sat up, suddenly intrigued. She disentangled her arm from mine and rested it on the table, propping up her chin in her hand. "Oh, this should be interesting." The way she eyed Seth was sort of challenging, as if she didn't quite believe he was about to tell her the honest truth. "Let's hear it."

"Listen carefully," he said. "I don't want to say this twice." After a quick survey of the room to gauge the potential for eavesdropping, he continued, "Underworld is the umbrella term. That encompasses everything, more or less. Which means the Underworld contains stuff like Hell and the weird purgatory you were in."

"So…that *wasn't* Hell," she mused.

"Didn't sound like it." Seth frowned. "There's plenty of shit living in Hell that would've been more than happy to talk to you for the rest of eternity. You know, bargain for your soul and things like that." He nodded toward me. "Logan's the one you want to talk to about cold, dark, and creepy."

I didn't deny it.

Veronica smirked. "What about Orion? He sleeps in dirt."

Seth barely managed to stifle a burst of laughter. His gaze moved straight to the vampire, who'd been uncharacteristically quiet up to now.

Orion rolled his eyes. "It's good for my skin." Then he added, "Contrary to popular belief, my darling, being a creature of night does not necessarily equal having an infernal nature. You're assuming Seth and I are of the same ilk, which is likely offensive to us both."

"Sorry. Slayer culture doesn't place a very heavy influence on differentiating between supernatural origin unless it has to do with specific weaknesses." She arched an eyebrow. "Just in case you forgot I'm supposed to be trained in how to kill all of you."

"I have to say, you're not doing a very good job." Whenever he spoke to V, Orion's voice lost some of its hard, habitually arrogant edge. He softened, and the thought occurred to me that perhaps this was what he was like before centuries of ruthless immortality took over.

"Let's just say my priorities shifted." Veronica winked. "As long as you're nice to me, that is."

We were interrupted by a waitress who promised to bring coffee and a mountain of pancakes. The conversation didn't immediately pick up again following her departure. I sensed a change in the atmosphere. Veronica's expression turned somber.

She said, "I wish you would be more accepting of Dylan. All of you." This time, her words weren't driven by an undercurrent of anger or spite. There was something else hiding below the surface, a deep, swirling pool of doubt. It dawned on me that she wanted us to approve of him so her own instincts could be quieted.

Seth shook his head firmly. "Sorry, honey. That's never happening." He had managed to develop a way of being blunt without being cruel, at least where Veronica was concerned. Aware of her feelings, and still completely immovable in his convictions.

"Why not?" She tried very hard to sound curious rather than petulant. Her heart rate had increased a little, her body noticeably tense. I gathered that this was a discussion she regretted as soon as it had begun.

"I can't tell you this without pissing you off." Seth leaned forward. "And I hate to be the bearer of bad news, but there's something messed up about him, V. Don't know what it is, but as long as I'm being honest, I don't want him anywhere near me or you."

She sucked in a deep breath. Her face was flushed. I could feel the heat radiating off her body. "That's not something you can just say about a person," she answered softly. "None of you understand what he's been through."

"Can I ask you something?" Seth spoke nonchalantly, as if we were talking about the weather.

"Sure." She lifted her chin slightly. We all knew

what that tiny motion meant; she was getting ready to dig in her heels.

"How long ago did he die?"

The question made me wince internally. All of a sudden, I could see exactly where Seth's line of thought was headed, and I wasn't sure I wanted to go down that road. A few minutes ago, we'd been ordering pancakes in peace. Was it too much to ask for that tranquility to persist for one morning? But the way things were, I knew it was. Better to get the difficult confrontations out of the way sooner rather than later. Or so I hoped, anyway.

Veronica shifted in the booth. "Years ago," she admitted, hesitating.

Seth looked at me. "That's what I thought. There's no way, babe. No way he came back completely intact. Several years is too much time."

Veronica was staring at me too, her pretty face reflecting fear and desperation. As I gazed down at her, I sensed something strange and powerful underneath her energy. I had felt an echo of it long before, back when we had first met. Now this power was much stronger, dominating her aura.

"Say something, Logan," she whispered.

What I wanted to say was that her time across the veil, however brief, had clearly stirred some unknown magic to awakening in her spirit. I wanted to say that I was almost positive this beautiful woman with the candy-colored hair was far more than she had originally appeared to be. And for her sake, I wanted to wholeheartedly disagree with Seth's assessment of her situation.

Unfortunately, I couldn't.

"The integrity of a soul can't be preserved forever in those in-between spaces," I said. "There's nothing to anchor them into the life they lost. They forget who they are, slowly at first, and then fast."

Unshed tears brightened her eyes. She pressed her lips together. "I don't want to talk about this right now. Not in public."

"That's fine." Seth leaned back. "It won't change my stance on the matter."

Orion shot him a glare, and he fell silent. A moment later, Veronica's phone vibrated against the tabletop. She picked it up, examined the screen, and sighed.

"It's Trent," she said. "Because of course it is."

"What's he want?" Orion fought an endless battle to seem neutral. Inside, we knew he was seething.

Veronica scanned the text. She chewed her lip, twirling a lock of hair around her finger. When she finally spoke, it was to me more than anyone else.

"He says Dylan wants to meet up later. He wants to see Lian too." Her worry proved impossible to mask. "What if she freaks out?"

"I wouldn't really blame her," I said.

"Neither would I, but..." Veronica let out her breath. "I guess I'm afraid she won't be happy."

Seth and Orion said nothing, but I could feel them listening.

"Why wouldn't she be, if you are?" I asked.

Veronica glanced away. "I don't know. And I hate that."

CHAPTER 16

SETH

J kind of felt like shit for stepping on V's feelings while we were supposed to be taking her to breakfast. It was not my intention to bullshit her, ever, but I couldn't help thinking about whether there might have been a better way to voice my concerns. *I should have left it to Logan, goddammit.* He was a man of few words, but they always seemed to be better than mine.

Nonetheless, what was done was done. We ate a ton of pancakes, paid the bill, and got the hell out of there, all without purposely breaching any more touchy subjects. But the specter of Dylan and what would happen when he saw him again lingered over everything, especially since he kept trying to arrange a meeting.

"He says he wants it to be like old times," V told

us. She furrowed her brow at the phone. "Him and Trent and Lian and me, just hanging out the way we used to every day."

"That makes it sound like we're not invited," I remarked.

"We must be," Orion interjected. For a moment, he was back to his old self, all stern and self-righteous. "I refuse to leave you alone with him." I hated that he was talking sense for once.

"We won't be alone," Veronica retorted. "Trent will be there, and so will Lian. You guys aren't the only ones who care about me, okay? I'm making my own choices whether you like it or not."

"You don't seem happy about it, though," Logan said.

She didn't answer him right away. I noticed her hand that was clutching the phone had gone white in the knuckles. "I'm just stressed." She ran her fingers through her hair. "At first, I was like, deliriously happy, but now..." Her voice trailed off. I watched her type something into her phone. The glow of the screen lit her features gently from below. Then she said, "He and Trent are going to see Lian by themselves. He wants me to meet up with them."

"That means you have two choices." I ticked them off on my fingers. "Either you can let us bug you so we can listen in, or we stake the place out in person."

"You have got to be kidding me," she muttered. She massaged her temples, as if attempting to ward off the mother of all headaches. "This is ridiculous."

"I don't think you mean that," Orion said.

"Oh yeah?" She scowled at him. "I'd love to know why."

He gazed at her evenly. "You haven't just left yet."

She covered her face with her hands. "Fucking hell. If I agree to this, you have to stay out of sight unless there's an emergency. A *real* emergency," she added pointedly. "Like, one of us has to be dying before you blow your cover. Understand?"

Orion grimaced, but he agreed. "As you wish."

"All right." She got up from the sofa and headed for the stairs. "Figure out your crazy plan. I need to get ready."

Once she was out of earshot, Orion and Logan turned to me. "This was your idea," the vamp declared. "You're taking point."

"Come on. Since when have I ever been the brains of an operation? You never had any problem taking over before." The truth was, I had no idea how to actually execute the terms of our agreement. Hell, she hadn't even told us where they were meeting.

"Times are changing fast," Orion replied. "Adapt or be left behind."

I grumbled. "Somehow you're still managing to be the fucking worst. Look, I was thinking we'd keep it as simple as we can. She goes to the meeting spot, we follow her to wherever that is, and then we keep real close tabs on his ass the whole time. I don't care if that fucker goes to take a dump. We need to be watching him."

Orion regarded me. "Do you know what he is, Seth? Your convictions against him are notable."

"It should be more than enough for you that he's back from the fucking dead, and he wants to be all over V. I do have a theory, though, now that you ask."

"Go on."

I detested the feeling of subordination Orion gave me, even when he wasn't meaning to. This time, however, I swallowed my objections and pressed on. In my head, I reminded myself over and over that Veronica meant more than nonsense bad blood between us. "I think he's a homunculus," I said. "Hollow. No soul. Like a puppet. Maybe he's fucking possessed, I don't know. But he's evil, and that's what matters here."

"Interesting." Orion steepled his fingers. "I believe he was resurrected by an as-yet-unidentified party. It would've had to have been a necromantic type of mage, and a powerful one at that. If he is a construct, he's well-made enough to fool Veronica. For now."

"What about you?" I said to Logan. "We shared our ideas. It's your turn."

He took his sweet time coming up with an answer, as usual. "I'm not quite sure," he said at last, "but the wendigo is key. I sensed its energy coming from the direction of downtown earlier. It isn't dead or gone." He paused. "And…Veronica changed while she was out of the mortal realm."

"Explain," Orion and I demanded simultaneously. I didn't like the sound of this at all.

"She has latent magical qualities that have remained dormant until now," Logan went on. "Beyond her capacity as a slayer and her associated training. What I felt was bound to her spirit. It's part of who she is." His calm, steady gaze moved to Orion. "You won't be able to turn her."

The vampire bristled. His veneer of tolerance cracked. "That's none of your concern," he said tightly. "I'll do with her what I please, provided she is in agreement."

I saw the opportunity to speak my mind on a

sensitive subject, and I took it. "You will ruin Veronica if you make her into one of yours, man. She wasn't meant to be a vampire." More than imagining her locked in creepy vampiric matrimony with Orion for the rest of time, it got under my skin to think of her alive, yet essentially lifeless, her soft skin drained of color and warmth.

"That is true," Logan reiterated. "It can't be done without risking disastrous consequences."

"This is an irrelevant tangent," Orion protested. "A distraction from the most important task at hand. I suggest we focus on our common enemy for the time being, rather than dividing ourselves." It wasn't the worst point he had ever made, and while I was certain he just wanted to get out of the hot seat, I let him off the hook.

"Fine. That's fair." I cleared my throat. "We'll talk about that other stuff later." He had no way of turning her without detection at the moment anyway. We had reached a tacit agreement to function more or less as a unit while Veronica was under threat. "As far as this asshole Dylan goes, I think the plan remains the same. They meet, we follow, he never leaves our sight." Anything more than that would be stepping on V's toes, and I still wanted to respect her. "Like she said, no intervention unless absolutely necessary."

Why did I have a feeling that absolute necessity was on the horizon?

"We can do that," Logan stated. Orion didn't seem quite as confident, but he permitted no resistance. He just folded his arms and nodded, one eye on the stairs, watching for V's reentry.

"We don't really have a choice," I said. "Our only other option is to trust the other slayer to keep her safe, and I don't know how I feel about that."

"No," Orion said. "We're going."

I grinned wryly. "And there it is."

An hour later, we were fanned out behind Veronica as she made her way to the meeting spot her friends had chosen—another restaurant, not far from the one we'd just been at. Before she approached the doors, she checked to make sure we were all in a suitable position; in other words, that she couldn't see us.

Don't worry about us, I told her. *We're fine. Get going.*

She frowned in my general direction, but a moment later she disappeared into the entryway.

Get up high, Orion said immediately. *Somewhere that will let you see inside.*

I moved around the perimeter, peering with sharp eyes through the huge, modern windows. It didn't take long to spot her hair tumbling out of the cap she had worn as she settled down at a table with three other people. The scene looked like an alternate universe recap of the morning. Except they were all tense from the start. It was almost like V had walked in on three people attempting to defuse a bomb.

You guys feel that? I asked. *What the hell was going on before we showed up?*

Orion's voice murmured in my head. *I don't like it.*

They don't trust him either, Logan said. *Especially the other girl.*

I zeroed in on her expression. She had a stone-cold poker face on. Not the way she should have looked just after reuniting with a long-lost friend. Her dark eyes stayed trained on Dylan with the intensity of a laser. She was ready for him to do something reckless, stupid, dangerous, or all of the above.

Hold on tight, I said, half to myself. *We might be about to go for a wild ride.*

CHAPTER 17

ORION

*V*eronica took a seat at that table, and the tension crackled through the air like electricity. We had split up to observe, but we all felt it as intensely as if we were sitting beside her. She must have sensed something too, because the first thing she did was look back and forth between the solemn faces of her friends.

The other girl, whom I assumed was the one known as Lian, acknowledged her with a quick, false smile. Her lips moved. I had to focus to hear her through the glass and the din of the other patrons.

"Hi, V. How are you feeling?" She spoke very deliberately, choosing each word with the utmost care. I got the strong impression that before

Veronica arrived, Lian had been navigating a precarious social minefield alone.

"Uh…fine." Again, Veronica looked around. "What's up with you guys? Are we going to a funeral after this?" She reached over and touched Dylan's arm. "How crazy is this, that we're all sitting at a table together somehow?"

He chuckled and shook his head. One of his hands found hers and squeezed it. "I gotta say, it's not something I ever imagined. I wished for it, when…" He trailed off, then cleared his throat. "Well, you know. And I can't believe my wish came true."

I turned my attention to Trent in an attempt to gauge his reaction. He sat back in his chair, saying nothing. His gaze traveled between every other person at the table. I could feel him thinking, mulling things over. The urge to jump in through the plate glass and ask him what he saw was nearly overwhelming.

As I watched the scene unfold, my hand curled into a loose fist. There was so much context I was plainly missing, cues I longed to understand. Was Dylan acting strangely? Had he said anything to arouse suspicion so far? What I really wanted to know was whether or not we'd be justified in leaping in and tearing him to shreds. Every inch of me itched to do just that.

If only such an intervention were possible! Nothing would have pleased me more, and it was a scenario at least Seth would also find agreeable. But Veronica had shown herself to be a naïve little fool in Dylan's presence; no doubt she'd be traumatized and start to despise me all over again. I couldn't bear the thought of losing her to the whim of mortal emotion, which meant I had no choice but to bite my tongue and bide my time.

"I'm sorry if I keep staring," Lian was saying. "I just can't wrap my head all the way around this yet. Where *were* you? How did you escape?" She paused. "How are you…alive?"

Even from a spectator's viewpoint, it was obvious that her questions made Veronica nervous. I watched my girl fidget subtly in her chair—touching her hair, turning the rings on her fingers, bouncing her knee gently underneath the tabletop. Was she anxious because she anticipated his answers and didn't want Lian to hear them?

Or maybe she feared what Dylan might say.

He better not slip up, Seth growled.

Personally, I wished he would. I wanted Veronica to see what she was choosing, to be forced to assess her own decisions without the rose-tint of nostalgia and lost love. Hints of who—or what—he truly was kept needling at me. She'd have to find out the truth sooner or later, and I had a feeling it wouldn't be pretty.

"It's hard to explain." Dylan talked calmly. He had an arm laid across the back of Veronica's chair, and every so often, his fingers grazed her shoulder. "I spent years just walking through an endless fog, with my memories drifting in and out. Sometimes I remembered myself, and I remembered you guys. But sometimes…nothing." He shrugged.

"That doesn't bother you?" Lian pressed. "Like, it's not hard to talk about now?" She looked over at Trent, possibly for backup, but he wouldn't take his eyes off Dylan. As if he expected his old friend to change into something unrecognizable at any moment.

Maybe he was smarter than I thought after all.

"I can't really explain that either." Dylan laughed, rubbing his forehead with the tips of his fingers. "It almost seems like a lifetime ago, even though I know it was literally yesterday. I guess my whole sense of time is messed up." He raised his eyes to stare at Lian. "How much does that matter? I'm here, aren't I?" The barest tinge of aggression colored his voice. He was apparently beginning to tire of the constant interrogation.

"Dylan, I'm not trying to be an asshole," Lian said immediately. "It's just…you came back from the dead. I think that matters a little bit."

"Yeah." Dylan took a deep breath and sat back. "You're right. Sorry. It's a shock for me too. I guess I have to adjust to the world of the living." He touched Veronica's shoulder and smiled when she looked his way. "I'd be lost if it wasn't for this girl right here."

Veronica smiled back. I felt her blush. "You're sweet," she said.

"Hey, I was thinking that maybe you and I could go out this afternoon," he added. "Just the two of us. Get some time alone." Somewhat sardonically, he addressed Trent, who still had not said a word. "Would that be okay with you, sir?"

Unamused, Trent frowned. "Not really."

"Come on." Dylan grinned, but there was a sharp edge forming on his demeanor. "Twenty-four hours of nonstop surveillance wasn't enough for you? I'm pretty sure if there was something wrong with me, it would've shown itself by now." He spread his hands on the table, palms up, to show they were empty. "Face it, bro. I'm back in business and there's nothing you can do about it."

The tone at the table had started to shift noticeably. The flavor of tension was turning slowly toward hostility. Trent's jaw was set hard as he regarded Dylan, his face expressionless.

"For what it's worth, I'd like that," Veronica said.

"See? Thank you, V." Dylan kissed her on the cheek. "It's what she wants, dude. We're all adults here. You can't just keep us locked away from each other until you're satisfied. We deserve a chance to reconnect."

There's no fucking way she's going anywhere alone with him, said Seth. *I'll climb a funeral pyre in the heights of Hell before I let that happen.*

Get ready to move, I replied. *In case they make a break for it.* I wanted to give Veronica the benefit of the doubt, that she wouldn't do something so reckless and stupid, but she could not be trusted to make wise decisions at the moment.

Oh, I'm ready. You there, angel-boy? Say something once a year so we know you're still with us.

They aren't leaving yet, Logan declared.

I refocused on the table, mostly to see if I could discern what the hell Logan was talking about. Lian sat with her chin propped on her hands, deeply pained. She couldn't stop scrutinizing Dylan. Suddenly, she sighed.

"You're not wrong," she admitted. "We wanted to make sure both of you were safe, that's all.

People don't just casually move back and forth across the veil."

"I know that, Li," Dylan answered. His speech was terse now. "And I appreciate your concern. But I'm fine. We're fine."

"Watch it," Trent warned. "Look, I get it. I don't care what you do on your own time, which starts now. But I'm going to be checking in pretty regularly for a while. And if you don't answer the phone I gave you, I'll come looking."

"All right, all right." Dylan gave up an annoyed little smirk. "Jeez. I didn't know things had changed this much while I was gone. I guess I can't really blame you." Dylan pushed his chair back and stood up. He stretched, but when Veronica went to join him, he stopped her mid-rise. "We'll get out of here in a sec, babe. I need to make a pit stop first."

Her eyebrows arched slightly. "Okay."

His smile turned as reassuring as he could make it. "Having my body back means I need to empty the tank again. I'll be right back."

She snorted. "Gross."

I watched her watch him walk away. As soon as he was out of earshot, Lian leaned over toward Veronica. She kept her voice so low I had to concentrate to make out the words.

"Don't take this the wrong way, but are you absolutely sure that's Dylan?"

"What are you talking about?" Veronica snapped. Her quick leap to Dylan's defense told me conclusively that she still had lingering doubts. "Who else could it be?"

"I don't know." Lian backed off. "Never mind." She exchanged a glance with Trent. "You're okay with going out with him alone? It won't be weird?"

"No. It feels amazing to be with him again," Veronica insisted. She kept peering restlessly in the direction Dylan had gone.

Someone needs to follow that bastard, Seth cut in. *Orion, it should be you. Logan and I will keep an eye on V.*

I grumbled under my breath. He was right, but I hated to let her out of my sight. Reluctantly, I peeled away from the main setting in the dining room to track Dylan's path away. To my surprise, I found that he had gone out a back exit and was standing in the shadow of a dumpster behind the restaurant.

I can't tell what he's doing, I said. *Stand by.*

But then a voice came through, like a radio picking up a stray channel. It was unclear whether he knew he could be heard, and the things he said set my teeth on edge.

"Renfrew," Dylan intoned. "I've got her. Tell the others it's time."

The moment I heard that name, all my patience, restraint, and sense flew out the window. His mention of a man called Renfrew filled me with hatred and resentment. The Renfrew I knew had been my friend long ago, but he'd defected from Anchorage on the promise of prestige further south.

Now, he sat on the clan council in Seattle, at the right hand of a mortal enemy. And this tainted boy was summoning them all back here.

The last thing I saw before being consumed by rage was Dylan's face turning toward me, painted with a mix of shock and sudden fear.

"What the f—?"

He was taking way too long to get back. For the first time since laying eyes on him, I started to get a little mad at Dylan. Here I was, trying my hardest to stick up for him and be understanding of his whole situation, and he paid me back by acting even weirder. It was getting more and more difficult to explain his behavior away, and I didn't like it.

Finally, I looked at Lian and voiced a suspicion that was taking root in my head. "The bathroom isn't over there, is it?"

I hadn't been talking to him, but Trent immediately shook his head. "It's over there." He nodded in the opposite direction, and when I looked, I could see the sign, clearly marked and not at all the way Dylan had headed. "I think we need to see what's up," Trent added.

"I'll go. Stay with Lian." He looked like he wanted to object, but changed his mind at the last minute, which I thought was wise. At this point, there was not a lot that could have kept me from finding out what the hell was up with Dylan. I hadn't thought there were many secrets to be gained in a plane of lightless purgatory. Maybe I was wrong.

The apprehension grew steadily on my way toward the back of the diner, where I thought he had gone. The feebly optimistic, lovesick corner of my consciousness tried to pretend I might encounter a previously hidden second bathroom that would make this all okay. Of course, I didn't find one. All I found was an exit leading straight out into the back delivery lot. And as I approached that door, I caught sight of two familiar figures wrestling viciously on the ground.

The moment my brain registered what my eyes were seeing, I let out a bloodcurdling scream that echoed out across the empty lot. Orion had Dylan pinned to the pavement, his knee pushed down into the center of Dylan's chest. One thought flashed like an emergency sign in my mind: *He's going to fucking kill him!* My fight instincts activated even before I stopped screaming.

"No!" Without a second thought, I threw myself into the brawl, grabbed Orion by the shoulders, and tried to yank him back. His head whipped around, fangs bared in a primal snarl. In that instant, I glimpsed a snapshot of the monstrosity that was evident to everyone else. He hardly looked like the man I had come to love.

He looked like what he was: a vampire.

"Stay out of this, Veronica," he hissed. "This part is none of your concern."

"Like hell it isn't! Get the fuck away from him!" Keeping one hand latched on to him, I reached into my pocket for my staff with the other. Whatever feelings I harbored for Orion evaporated away in the face of furious betrayal. He *knew* how much Dylan meant to me, conflicted or not, and this was the choice he had made?

"Veronica!" Orion roared. He snatched the front of my shirt, tearing through the fabric, and shoved me backward. "Stop!" He glowered at me. "You know nothing, and you will only get hurt."

"Oh yeah?" I balanced on my back foot. The staff extended with a snap. I brandished it at him. "You know what? Fuck off. I thought you actually wanted what was best for me and didn't know how to express it. But now I see you're just fucking jealous because someone you've never met is suddenly more deserving of my attention."

On the ground, Dylan took the opportunity to shove Orion's knee off his chest. I reached out my hand; he grabbed it and got to his feet. Then he looked at me strangely, head cocked to the side.

"Jealous?" he said. "Why would he be jealous, V? He's a vamp."

I realized too late that I had let slip some pretty heavy inferences to the true nature of my relationship with Orion. And because Dylan was not a total idiot, he began to do the math pretty fast. Orion just eyed us both in silence. He, too, seemed aware that the game had changed, and he was just waiting to see what his next move had to be.

"You didn't notice he came to Denali to rescue me?" I asked Dylan, maintaining a tough exterior. *Don't back down, don't show weakness, don't look scared.* The three of us were a house of cards now, swaying in a dangerous wind. *This is not my fault.*

Obviously, that was a lie. This could not have been any more my fault than it already was.

Dylan's confusion morphed into shock and anger. I watched the emotions roll across his face like an unstoppable tide. "You were with him," he said softly. "He's jealous because you have fucking *been* with him and he thinks you're his!" The volume of his voice started to climb. "How could you?"

And just like that, the house of cards came down.

"Dylan, I—"

He didn't let me get more than those two words out. "No. Fuck no, V. I cannot fucking believe that you came to find me, and then you brought me back, into a world where you're riding a vampire's dick. Tell me it's not true, I'm literally begging you. Tell me this is all some crazy prank, and I'm gonna wake up at home in Seattle like nothing ever happened. Can you tell me that?"

I couldn't, and I couldn't bring myself to confirm what he now knew, so I kept my mouth shut.

He scowled. "I really wanted a future with you, Veronica. When I was walking alone in that place for God knows how long, the memories of you were the ones that returned the most. Of us together. They were my only escape from the void." He stared at me, his eyes abruptly hollow. "How could you do this to me?"

The lump in my throat was too big to speak around. Every muscle in my face had gone taut with the Herculean effort it took not to collapse in tears. "I'm sorry," I whispered. "This isn't what I meant to happen."

"Disgusting." He clenched his jaw. "Do you hear me? You're disgusting! I died, and after all this time, you didn't learn a fucking thing! I thought you were better than this, Veronica. I thought you were smarter."

The hot tears welling in my eyes finally spilled over. I held his searing gaze for as long as I could, but eventually the pain grew overwhelming, and I had to look away. As my head turned, I saw the back door of the restaurant opening to let Trent into the lot. He was quickly followed by two others —Seth and Logan. They stopped in their tracks for just long enough to assess the shitshow unfolding before their eyes. Then they broke into a run toward us.

"Really? You've got nothing to say?" Dylan's voice had taken on a taunting edge. "You're not even going to look at me anymore? That's pathetic." He chuckled grimly. "And to think, I almost defied all my orders for you."

The entire world stopped for me when he said that. I glanced up in slow motion, all sounds muted under a foggy hush in my ears. My lips and tongue moved, but it seemed like a long time before I heard the word that emerged from my mouth.

"What?" I blinked, again in slow motion. "What are you talking about?"

Someone yelled, "Get out of here, V!" But I wasn't able to listen, or even process what was being said. The jarring revelation Dylan had dropped on me was rooting my feet to the faded pavement. Our eyes were locked.

"That voice I told you about," Dylan said. "The one that told me the doorway out was going to appear after we found each other." A slight smile curved his lip. "He's the one who made it all possible."

"V!" I recognized the shouting as coming from Seth this time. He leapt in front of me, temporarily blocking my view of Dylan. "God damn, girl, you got a death wish or what?" he demanded. He grabbed me by the shoulders. "Get the fuck out of here before I throw your ass out. Go somewhere safe. We'll deal with this."

"No." I put my hands on his chest and pushed. "Let us finish talking. I need to find out what's going on here or it'll haunt me for the rest of my life."

Seth hesitated. He growled. "Fine. But he makes one false move, and we're killing him on the spot. I don't want to do that in front of you."

I sure as hell didn't want that either, but the

notion of leaving without closure was unbearable. Seth stepped aside, and I looked at Dylan. "Can you just fucking cut it out with this cryptic bullshit and tell me the truth?"

"Why?" he asked. "I just found out you've been lying to me this whole time. Are you fucking all of them, V? Is that why they follow you around like some kind of messed-up entourage?" He sighed. "Honestly, maybe it's my fault for assuming you'd still be the girl I knew and loved. How easily we forget the ones we've lost, right?"

Every word was like a knife in my heart. "I never forgot you," I murmured.

"Lies!" Dylan exploded in a sudden bout of rage. "You're a fucking liar!" He lunged toward me, his face grotesquely contorted. The next thing I knew, the others had brought him down hard onto the ground at my feet. One of Seth's claws hovered at Dylan's throat.

"You fucked up big-time, kiddo," the demon said.

Dylan's face went blank, but only for a second. Then he started laughing, almost hysterically. The sound spiraled up from the parking lot into the sky, soaring out over the city. I knew I'd never be able to forget it.

"Me?" He was still laughing so hard that tears

pooled at the corners of his eyes, and he had to catch his breath. "I'm not the one who fucked up." He nodded in my direction. "She is. She just doomed every single one of you." To Orion, he said, "Especially you, asshole."

My stomach dropped. I felt horribly sick. How *could* I have done this? And yet, I was unable to separate the seething, bitter person in front of me from the Dylan I'd known for so long. He still felt the same, in ways that really mattered.

But not even my lovesick heart could deny what was happening. Seth held Dylan's head up by his hair, one demon claw poised and ready. I kept waiting for him to pierce the skin, for the blood to start flowing and never stop.

Instead, they all waited.

Seth's eyes were riveted on me. "Say the word, or don't."

I knew that I should have instructed them to kill Dylan. Deep down, I understood that I had been fooled. No matter what I longed for, he was not the same. My Dylan would have died before he hurt me—in fact, he already had.

But I just couldn't bring myself to pull the metaphorical trigger.

"Spare him," was what came out. "Please. Until we can figure this out."

Seth wanted to protest. I could see how badly he wanted to defy me, and how wrong he thought I was. Truthfully, there was nothing stopping him except his own restraint, which he exercised. The claw was withdrawn from Dylan's neck. I breathed a sigh of sorrow, frustration, defeat, and relief.

Trent was the one who stepped forward to break the new silence. He gazed down at Dylan for a few long moments.

"Get up," he said. "Start talking. This is your only chance to tell us everything."

"And if I don't?" Dylan asked. His nerve pissed me off at the same time it appealed to my senses. I wished he hadn't just shattered my vision of him, for many reasons.

Trent shifted to reveal the long, cruel blade holstered at his waist. "Then I guess we might never know."

"Trent." I shot him a desperate, pleading look.

"Let him up," Trent said to Orion and his crew. Still restrained, Dylan staggered to his feet. A bruise was blooming on the side of his face that had been pressed to the ground. He and Trent glared at each other. "Speak," Trent ordered. "Now."

CHAPTER 19

LOGAN

We made an impromptu circle around Dylan in the back lot behind the restaurant, a shield between him and the civilized mortal world. His eyes, flat and filled with mockery, stayed pinned on Trent, though I knew he could feel us all watching. He must have known, too, that we were primed to remove him from the mortal realm at a moment's notice—and we weren't inclined to be merciful. If not for Veronica, he probably would have been reduced to a corpse already.

Still, he smiled. A cruel smile, but one none-theless. Part of me had to admire the absolute gall it had to take to grin in the face of four beings who didn't much care if he lived or died. But more than that, I was annoyed by him, by the things he'd done and the time he'd stolen.

We should have killed him on the mountain, I lamented.

Seth replied, *No shit.*

"Okay, look." Dylan tried to free his arms from Seth's grip and was met by a ruthless jerk of the shoulders that forced him to grimace in pain. "Here's the deal. Remember I mentioned that voice? He told me he was a shaman working for a guy in Seattle named Steele. I didn't get much more than that, but I mean, I've been around the block once or twice, right? I can recognize a vamp when I hear about one."

Orion let out a low, barely restrained growl. His eyes blazed. The thin veneer of humanity slipped away from his visage once more. "He sent you?"

"Maybe. I don't know who the fuck it really was, to be honest. And I don't care. The only thing I cared about was that I'd get to see Veronica." He paused. "Yeah, they told me to get rid of her, but up until now, I was undecided. Hell, I just told you I was about to throw it all away."

Veronica gasped. I glanced at her. She had a hand over her mouth, tears rolling silently down her cheeks.

"You changed your mind?" Trent asked. His stance and tone were both deceptively casual; his energy ran tense and hot like a live wire. He was prepared, like we all were, for anything.

"Well, yeah." Dylan turned his head to the side and spat on the pavement. "Obviously. Why should I give a fuck about what happens to a traitor?"

Veronica sank to her knees. On Dylan's right, Seth glowered, digging his claws into the flesh of the captive's arm and shoulder. A dark patch of blood began to bloom around new wounds, black instead of fresh red.

"Watch your mouth," Seth snarled.

Dylan laughed. "Oh, it's probably too late for that." Although he continued to jockey for advantageous positioning, he seemed completely unaffected by physical pain. The bruise around his eye was darkening rapidly, giving one side of his face a strange, almost skeletal appearance. "I've summoned the rest. They're coming. If you're lucky, it will be a matter of days—and this time there will be no one to stop them."

"You don't know that!" Orion barked.

Dylan looked at him with the same flat, baleful expression. "Tell me I'm fucking wrong," he retorted calmly. "Tell me it isn't just you and these two rejects sitting here in this shithole city, just waiting to be finished off for good. I saw what happened to your followers, man. All the bodies. The carnage." Another chuckle escaped his lips. "I bet you thought you were safe in the forest."

Orion was briefly stunned into silence. Seth and I exchanged a glance. A seed of realization had begun to grow in my mind. I wondered if anyone else could tell that I was starting to understand. The undercurrent of death and darkness surging through Dylan's energy. The trail of the wendigo leading downtown to exactly the area in which we now stood.

"How do you know about that?" Veronica's voice, subdued and shaken, struggled to be heard. She sat numbly on the ground, staring up at Dylan. A thousand raw emotions stormed across her face, sorrow shifting into disbelief, shifting into anger, and back again.

He scoffed. "And you call yourself a slayer? You were there! You were in it! I shouldn't have to explain this to you." He let out a pitying sigh. "But I will, for old times' sake. Not like I've got anything else to do. My job here is almost done."

"Hurry up," Trent ordered. His patience was running thin.

Dylan rolled his eyes. "Fine. So that thing, whatever it was, that tore your little clan apart?

That was plan A, and it worked pretty well until little Miss V came along and tossed in a big old wrench. She would've been a problem if my shaman friend hadn't found a way to make her into a solution instead." His grin widened. "The shaman saw her for what she was: a massive weakness even after the rest of the clan had been obliterated. And so, plan B was born."

"Let me guess," Trent said. "That's you."

The gears that had been turning in my brain finally clicked into place. I could practically see it happening, the ritual binding Dylan's spirit together from scraps of dark and potent energy. Some from the shaman himself, some from Veronica's enduring memories, and some from the wendigo I had so helpfully restored to full health hours before chasing it to the peak of Denali.

That was why Veronica had to die—so that Dylan could live once more. She had been part of the fuel that stoked the fire of his spirit and propelled it back into the corporeal realm. The wendigo had disappeared after playing its part in the resurrection, its energy spent into nothingness.

But Veronica had endured. Not only that, she had somewhat thrived.

"Yours truly," Dylan announced with pride. "Poised to strike the killing blow, whatever it took.

At first, I thought I'd just steal her away. Make her mine again and we'd live happily ever after." His face darkened. "But, no." He spoke directly to her. "You can fucking rot."

In the grand scheme of things, this last little jab wasn't much, a parting shot on the heels of a much greater betrayal. But for Orion, it was the last straw. He roared, lunging at Dylan in a dark flash of fangs and claws. Before Seth or I had time to react, slashes of scarlet ripped across the boy's face, narrowly missing his open eyes.

"Don't you dare speak to her!" Orion was nearly foaming at the mouth. "Not now. Not again. Not ever!" He went to seize Dylan by the throat, presumably to choke the life from him. But as it turned out, Dylan had other plans. Quick as lightning, he managed to tear himself free of Seth's grasp and shove Orion back. Caught off guard by the boy's apparent strength, Orion stumbled backward, catching himself on the asphalt.

"You want to dance, old man?" Dylan taunted. "C'mon. Let's dance." He swooped in low, driving his shoulder into Orion's midsection. Seth and I observed in silence for a few moments as the two of them peppered each other with a flurry of blows.

"We should help," I remarked casually.

"Not yet." Seth smirked. "For once, my money's on the vamp, but I want to see where this goes."

It didn't take very long to find out. Frustrated and nearing the point of blinding rage, Orion began to falter a little. He let himself get pinned in a corner of the lot, half on his back, braced against the full brunt of Dylan's onslaught. The remains of a broken bottle gleamed in Dylan's hand. He raised it high.

"Okay." Seth stepped forward. "Orion's about to get shredded. Now we intervene." The bottle embarked on a swift descent. At any moment, I expected to hear an incensed shriek of pain from our previously insurmountable leader. As before, I felt sorry for him. No one understood the pain of a fall from such high grace better than me.

But the shattering impact never came. Dylan's body jerked to a sudden stop, frozen in an unnatural position. Closing the distance behind Seth, I came up beside Orion and realized that he had plunged the claws on both hands deep into Dylan's chest. Adrenaline-fueled fury coursed through his body.

Dylan grinned, his teeth stained with blood. "Touché," he said. Less than a second later, Orion surged upward, hurling him through the air. His body made a hollow metallic sound as he struck the side of a dumpster.

Off to the side, Veronica shuddered. She hadn't said a word in five or ten minutes. Her cheeks were wet with tears. I moved toward her but was interrupted by Seth's voice.

"What the hell are you looking at?" he demanded brusquely. Too late, I spotted the small crowd that had gathered at the restaurant's back door.

"You got a lot of nerve, buddy," said a man at the front. "And you're gonna need it, 'cause the cops are on their way."

Seth spat; it sizzled on the pavement. "God-dammit," he muttered. "All right, all right. Let's go, you sons of bitches." He turned away from the back wall of the restaurant toward the dumpster where Dylan had fallen just in time to see the boy spring up and make a break for it. "Over my dead fucking body!" he barked.

We chased him together like a pack of wolves, some hungrier than others. Even Trent ran along, though I couldn't tell if he was in pursuit of Dylan, of us, or all of the above. Suddenly, the alliance we had forged on the peak of Denali seemed extra fragile, stretched thin by circumstance. What would happen between predators once we'd caught up with the prey?

Ultimately, Orion was the one who took him down—and fittingly so, since his temper flared the hottest. By the time Dylan came skidding to a halt, right on the edge of where the grass met the tree line, his shirt was a bloody tangle of cloth. He lay there, defiant even as he panted for breath, staring up at us with baleful eyes.

Seth planted a foot squarely in the middle of the would-be fugitive's back. "Nice try."

Dylan let out a slightly strained chuckle. "Worth a shot."

Orion withdrew his claws. "Take him back to the house. I'm going to get Veronica."

"I don't think so," Trent said.

Orion didn't hesitate. "I don't care," he answered. "He won't be allowed out of my sight until he is no longer a threat. Take that as you will—it's non-negotiable." He kept walking toward the parking lot, where I could still see Veronica sitting on the ground. "Your bond with him is obvious," Orion added. "Sooner or later, you'll give in to the past, as Veronica did."

Trent frowned. "No. Allegiance isn't the problem." He caught up with Orion and put his hand on his shoulder to stop him. "I don't want him returning to Seattle. We all know there's another fight brewing. You could lose track of him."

"You think me a fool, slayer?" Orion scoffed.

Trent smirked. "You know, it's actually hilarious that you think I, a *vampire slayer*, am somehow cool with Clanmaster Steele getting everything he wants." He ran a hand through his hair. "I'll admit, I'd rather not see Dylan murdered in front of my eyes again. But for once in both our lives, I'm not trying to double cross you here. I just won't give up custody of a dangerous fugitive to someone with whom there is no trust."

"He's coming to the house," Orion declared flatly. "And so is Veronica."

Trent sighed. "Listen, all I want is a promise that you're not gonna give me back a corpse. This is tough for a guy like you to understand, but Veronica and Lian and I are human, and so was Dylan at one point. We aren't like you in the way that you watch mortal lifetimes go by in the blink of an eye. We need closure. We need to know answers. We don't have all the time in the universe to get them. And we won't get shit if Dylan's dead."

Orion looked back at him, mulling over his words. I looked at Trent and wondered if he understood everything about Veronica after all. He spoke about her as though, at the end of the day, she was fragile and her time was limited. To be fair, I could see how he might make such assumptions. She'd been gravely injured in recent days. She had bled, and she'd need to recover.

But I no longer fully believed that Veronica was a mortal woman, or even just a slayer. Something previously unseen within the depths of her aura had started to bloom when she moved across the veil.

Maybe no one else knew it yet, but she had come back changed.

CHAPTER 20

SETH

As good as it felt to finally release some of the urge for violence that had been pent up inside me for days, I knew implicitly that we'd fucked up. Our mistakes were written large in Veronica's thousand-yard stare, in the dull silence she maintained while we fled the scene of the brawl. The sirens approaching down the street couldn't follow us into the trees, and so they never quite caught up. I listened to them circle a few times, then fade.

We marched our captive through the woods, two in front and two behind—and V trailing after. She didn't want to come within ten feet of the weaselly bastard, but I saw her sneaking glances his way every now and then. The tears on her face had dried, and yet she looked as if she might erupt with new ones any second.

It was the first time I had ever seen her look anything close to fragile. I hated it, and I hated him for singlehandedly stealing her strength and confidence, however temporarily. Of course she'd get her damn groove back, but the fact she'd lost it at all was unforgivable.

Thirty feet from the house, Trent stopped the caravan. He stared Dylan in the eyes for a long moment, then turned to Orion. "Keep him for now," he said. "Not a scratch, and I'll bring you reinforcements to use against Seattle. Just like we agreed. Yeah?" In a show of good faith, he pushed Dylan toward the vamp and actually stepped back.

I had to give it to the guy; for a mortal, he sure was ballsy. Nothing was stopping Orion from grabbing the kid and ripping his throat out right where he stood. He wanted to—I knew that much beyond a shadow of a doubt.

Orion's face had been fixed in a permanent scowl ever since we escaped downtown. Now he aimed it at Trent. "Fine. Retrieve your woman and go. We will safeguard this…thing." He gestured to Dylan.

Trent started to nod and stopped partway through. "Don't talk about Lian like that," he said.

"Take care of V. And keep them away from each other."

I laughed. "Oh, don't worry. He ain't going nowhere."

After that, Trent was gone, retracing his steps back to downtown. We had left the girl he clearly cared for more or less to fend for herself, and I felt kind of bad about that.

"Put him in the cellar," Orion said. He went to V, slipping an arm gently around her waist. She sort of sagged into him. Her skin was paler than usual; even her vibrant hair seemed to have lost some of its color. When his gaze fell on her, the darkness dominating his face gave way to worried tenderness so obvious that not even I could deny his feelings. "I need to take her inside," he said quietly.

"Yeah, yeah. Go on." I reached over and grabbed the prisoner by the collar. "I'll take first watch with this shitty piece of work." To Logan, I said, "You too. Don't worry about us. We'll be fine." I paused. "Or at least I will be."

"You heard the deal Orion made with the slayer," Logan replied serenely. "Not a scratch." He headed for the house, leaving me alone with my new best friend.

"Damn," Dylan muttered. "What's it take to get

a rise out of that guy?"

I steered him toward the cellar doors. "More than you've got, asshole."

He didn't fight me on the way down the stairs. Maybe it was the way the place smelled—of damp and dirt, and a little bit like death. As a man who had come from beyond the veil, I hoped he could tell exactly what had happened here. *When you close your eyes, I hope you see us dumping that body into the inlet. Because with any luck, you'll be next.*

"Nice digs," Dylan remarked, glancing around. I suspected his nonchalant manner was little more than a bluff, though he voiced no outward complaints when I bound him and sat him against a pillar.

"Get used to 'em," I said. "Don't think you'll be seeing anything else of the city for a while."

"We'll see." He leaned his head back on the stone, staring up at the cobwebbed rafters. I went and closed the cellar doors, and the light shrank down to thin, pale slivers slicing across our faces. A hush descended. I could hear things skittering over the walls and the floor every now and then.

The sound made me wonder how long it'd take for the kid to crack. He talked a pretty mean game, and he knew it. But he had been human once. A human with mortal fears. I watched him out of the corner of my eye as seconds grew into minutes, inching slowly toward an hour. A quarter of the way there, he began to fidget. It was subtle; tapping of the fingers, the restless bouncing of the knee. I tried not to smile.

Finally, he spoke up into the quiet gloom. "What'd he have to promise to get you on his side?" Dylan didn't specify a name, but he didn't have to.

"None of your business," I answered easily. "But it *is* my business to ask you the same question. What are *you* getting out of this deal?"

Dylan smiled grimly. He dropped his head, grinning at the floor between his feet. The small space of the cellar seemed to amplify his unnatural energy.

"I thought I was getting Veronica," he admitted. "Or at least another chance to see her. And I guess if you want to be real technical about it, I did get that." He shook his head. "It wasn't supposed to be like this, though. I had a whole vision in my head of what was going to happen once I got back into a real body."

I folded my arms and leaned on the wall. "How's that working out for you?" The kid's eyes glinted.

"It's not," he muttered.

"Not to rub salt in the wound, but I could've

told you it wouldn't. Any one of us could, including your friends. That's the crazy thing about the mortal realm. Nothing ever fucking shakes out like you think it will."

"That's easy for you to say." Dylan turned his head toward me. His gaze bored into mine, cold and steely. "You ever been anywhere worse than here?"

My mind flashed back to the Underworld, cold seeping through my bones as I walked blindly through the dark. "Yeah, actually I have. Thanks for asking. It doesn't make the things I just said any less true."

Dylan stared at me. The more I looked at him, the more convinced I became that he was hollow, missing something crucial. Whoever this mystery vamp shaman was, he hadn't gotten the resurrection ritual quite right.

A sudden thought made my skin prickle. *Unless this is what he wanted.*

"Then you should know what it's like to be in a place like that." All the casual levity had gone out of Dylan's manner in the blink of an eye. I had never seen a man in his predicament look so serious. "I forgot everything about who I was or who I had been. I felt it all slipping away, and there was nothing I could do." He paused. "Eventually, V was all I had left. My scattered memories of her, old feelings, her face…" His voice trailed off, then picked back up. "She was the only thing anchoring me to a shred of sanity."

"She thought you were dead," I reminded him.

"She wasn't wrong." He kept staring at me, practically unblinking. "But I wasn't gone either. I was just there enough to know she was on the other side of this wall keeping us apart. And to tell you the truth, I would've agreed to anything if she was the reward. In life, and in death."

"Huh." I arched my eyebrows. "She's certainly unique, and I don't know that I can entirely fault your logic, but…you've been taken for a ride." He was silent, so I continued. "There's no way in hell this shaman ever intended to make good on whatever he said to you. He works for a guy who'd like nothing more than to see Orion moldering in the ground. You gave them a way to try and make that happen." I stopped talking to let my words sink in. "Because you're an idiot."

The kid scowled. "I had a plan to double-cross them before they got a chance to fuck me over. As long as I had Veronica with me, it didn't matter if we were on the run for the rest of our lives. The important thing was that we'd have the rest of our lives in the first place."

A chuckle escaped my lips. "Pretty big dream for a guy who shouldn't exist at all. The way I see it, you ought to be killed. And if that doesn't work, you ought to be killed again." I glanced over. He wasn't looking at me. "How much of your old self do you think you really are?"

He shrugged awkwardly, the movement stunted by the bindings around his hands. "Honestly, I thought I was perfect when we first came through the doorway on Denali. The vibe was a little off, but that made sense. It's not like I was gone for a day or two and came back as if nothing happened." His expression darkened. "But then she let slip that she's been fucking around with you guys, and—" He sighed. "The rage wasn't normal, man."

"Let me guess." I smirked wryly. "You were never a violent person before."

"Well, it sounds stupid as hell when you say it like that, but I really wasn't. And yet at the same time, I mean, she betrayed me and everything I stood for while I was alive. I was martyred by a vampire, and here she is screwing one?" His face contorted into a mask of frustration. "I don't fucking understand it. Don't I have a right to be pissed off?"

"No," I told him without hesitation.

"Oh, please." He smiled. "I'd love to hear you explain this to me."

"Okay, fine." I straightened up. "This idea that she betrayed you is utter bullshit. Yeah, it blows that you were trapped in a horrible, timeless pocket of the ether, but guess what, buddy? Veronica wasn't! She was left to pick up the pieces and move on without you, because she had no choice. She didn't want to. She wasn't over it. She was just forced to keep going."

"The V I knew would never have jumped in bed with a goddamn vamp," Dylan insisted. "Especially not if she was going around calling herself a slayer."

"Then I guess you don't know her anymore," I said. "It's been a long time, kid. You can't expect her to stay exactly the same."

He was quiet for a few moments. Then he laughed. "What am I doing? You're a fucking monster, dude. You don't know anything about love."

"Maybe I don't. But I will not allow you to destroy Veronica's life all over again." My eyes locked with his. His restless leg stopped moving.

"That's noble of you," Dylan replied dismissively. "Too bad it's already too late."

ORION

What I wanted was to get Veronica inside the house without letting her see her little boyfriend get carted off to the cellar by Seth. But she was uneasy, and she wouldn't stop looking around, as much as I tried to keep her on a straightforward path. She glimpsed them veering off toward the cellar doors, Dylan's arms twisted behind his back in chains.

She looked at me then. "What are you going to do with him?"

"That depends on how he behaves," I said. In truth, I didn't really know yet. I did know, however, that if I showed a hint of weakness, she would feel it. Her unusually sharp perception was always there, despite how badly her world had just been shaken. I felt sympathy for her, and perhaps even empathy. I had suffered similarly, a long time ago. It was a kind of pain I no longer experienced, but the memory remained.

Veronica sighed. "Here's the part where I want to ask you not to kill him. A few hours ago, I might have begged, if that's what you really wanted." She dropped her gaze as I stopped to unlock the front door. "Now...I don't think I understand anything anymore."

I hesitated. The lost, raw vulnerability in her voice forced the realization to dawn upon me that we were crossing into uncharted territory. The familiar dynamic to which I'd become accustomed had changed. To my chagrin, there was no plan for that either.

Instead of swallowing my pride and admitting I was at a loss, I placed my hands on her shoulders, turned her gently to face me, and said, "Tell me what you need, Veronica. I'm here for you, and I will do my best."

She smiled a little. A spark of humor lit her pale eyes briefly. "Wow. That sounds a lot like compassion coming from you." Veronica reached up and wrapped her arms around my neck. She pressed her lips to my cheek. "Thank you."

I held her tightly. The urge to never let go was almost overwhelming. "I'm sorry that my actions in the parking lot upset you." I knew, implicitly, that I needed to apologize for something but couldn't bring myself to repent for the attack. As far as I was concerned, Dylan needed to be expunged from the realm sooner rather than later.

She smiled again, slightly wider. "Well, I'm proud of you for saying that." Then her gaze focused on a point over my shoulder. I should have known what was coming. "But you know what I need right now?" Her hand came to rest on my chest. "I need to be alone with Logan for a while."

Like I said, I should have known. She needed tender calm, two things I had rarely been over the course of our relationship. My love for her was wildly passionate, a storm of naked desire. Still, the request took me by surprise. I wasn't able to fully conceal the sting.

"That is not what I thought you would say," I told her. "Speaking in the interest of total honesty."

"I know." She inched me away, loosening my grasp on her waist. "But you asked, so I answered. I promise it's nothing personal."

"All right." The warmth I'd gotten from holding her quickly turned into a jealous ache. I turned away before she went to Logan so that I wouldn't have to see him take my place. He didn't say a word, and strangely, I envied that too. The stillness in his manner—that was why she wanted him now instead of me.

Why can't I be everything to her?

The thought came out of nowhere, and it left me physically unsettled, as if I had just been shocked. I pushed it down until the door of my chambers was closed and locked at my back. She was leading me down a dangerous road that skirted the edge of mortal emotion too closely for my liking. The mistake of loving a human too deeply was one I'd already made. And so was the catastrophic error of making my lover into my thrall.

And yet, the hunger to possess her gnawed at my eternal bones. I feared that it would never leave me, no matter where Veronica was or what she was doing. I could not fathom an immortal life of such intense yearning.

"I want to turn her," I muttered out loud. Hearing the words strengthened my resolve. "No, I have to turn her." A soft, doubting internal voice reminded me how Logan and Seth said it wasn't possible, that I'd ruin her. I would have been lying to say their reservations didn't concern me, at least more than they had in the past. But they failed to quell my desire.

There were greater things standing in the way

of my ambition, namely the inevitable return of the Seattle clan. If I turned inward for long enough, I could sense the storm brewing on the horizon. They were far away at the moment, but that wouldn't buy us much time. Once the march began, it would be fast and relentless.

I knew it was only a matter of time. Under these circumstances, Veronica should have been little more than a second thought, a distraction to be saved for later. In theory, I had more important things to worry about. In practice, the only way I could tear her out of my thoughts was acknowledging that the Anchorage clan teetered on the edge of extinction. Everything I had worked for generations to build would be washed away like sandcastles in the tide.

Focus, fool! I closed my eyes, inhaled deeply, and cleared my mind as much as I was able to. The clarity I received was a dismal reality; my sole remaining option seemed to be a path I never would have chosen to take of my own free will. Step one—the uneasy truce with the human slayer Trent was already in place, however tenuously. I hoped that our alliance would be enough to sustain the lifeblood of the clan.

Step two was a little more complicated. Dylan's capture gave me a secret trump card for as long as it could be kept undiscovered by Seattle's prying eyes. I paced the length of my room, wishing I'd thought to interrogate him about the nature of his connection to Steele and his council of elders. If they could see him at will, I might already have been screwed; no doubt they'd want their mole back.

But if they remained ignorant for a while longer, I fully intended to use the boy as a bargaining chip to gain leverage in what I had to admit was a fairly one-sided debate. Someone higher in their ranks saw Dylan as a key to success, perhaps a tool that would allow them to kill Veronica and me with the same stone. And in that respect, he was undeniably a liability, which made him valuable to everyone involved.

Much as I detested the very ground he walked upon, Dylan was our sole advantage in the impending fight. It pained me deeply to leave so much of the clan's future in the reactionary hands of the enemy, but I was backed up to the edge of a cliff, one foot planted on thin air. The days of playing life like a chess game, always one move ahead, were behind me now.

The vampires of Anchorage had been culled, and then we became the hunted. There was nothing left to do except ensure that we did not lay down and die at the feet of our adversaries. And for the first time in a very long time, I had something other than power hunger and bloodlust fueling my determined rage.

Veronica had given me a cause. I would fight for my clan, of course, for our lands, and for my status as its rightful master. But I would also fight for her. Because she deserved everything that Steele and his army sought to take away.

CHAPTER 22

VERONICA

"Wow," I said under my breath as Orion's footsteps faded up the stairs. "He actually left." I crossed into the den and sat down on the overstuffed arm of the couch, half-expecting to hear him turn around and come running back in a fit of jealous fury.

"There's been some self-improvement happening." Logan sat on the sofa beside me, his shoulder brushing my back. The ethereal shadow of his right wing touched between my shoulder blades, and my body released an involuntary shudder of something very close to pleasure. How was it that any one of these men had the power to awaken lust in me, no matter what else was happening? Orion could have done it too, but Logan was the one I needed. He was gentler than the other two, steady and calm. The rock in a vicious storm.

"Huh." I turned halfway and slung my arm across the angel's shoulders. "I didn't think he had it in him, honestly."

"We'll see." Logan smiled slightly. "It's incremental, so far." He caught my hand in his, kissed the back of it, and pulled me down into his lap. I landed sideways, my head nestled against the left side of his collarbone. He brushed some of my hair out of his face. "How are you feeling?"

"Ugh." I curled up in his arms. "I don't even know. It's like, on one hand I could write a fucking book about my emotions right now. But on the other…it wouldn't make any sense, because they're all messed up." I sighed. "Being human is stupid."

"Yeah." He stroked my hair idly. "What about being half human?"

I laughed. "I wouldn't know. I don't think being a slayer counts as a racial identity."

"That's not what I'm talking about." Logan lifted his left arm a little to prop me up higher. "Remember when we met in the woods and I did this?" He leaned in and kissed me on the lips. From the way he'd led into it, I thought it would be more or less chaste, but there was an undercurrent of sensuousness that would've made my knees weak if I wasn't already in his lap.

When he pulled away, I sat stunned for a second or two before realizing that my vision had changed. Energy swirled in the air, encompassing both of us in glowing auras. Over Logan's shoulder, I spotted an indistinct figure strolling past the doorway. The air in that direction turned cold.

A spirit, whispered a new, small voice in my ear.

"Oh yeah. Does Orion know his house is haunted?"

Logan shrugged. "I doubt it. He probably would have made me chase them all out." He looked at me. "See how that works, though?" I nodded, and he added, "It's not supposed to."

"What do you mean?" I asked. "You don't do this with every girl you meet at a crime scene in the forest?"

"Not every human girl," he replied. "Mortals weren't made to house power like that in their bodies. That's why they're mortals." With the patience of a saint, he watched my face, waiting for me to get it.

I frowned. "Okay. But I mean, I have slayer's blood now, so I'm not technically human. It still makes sense."

"The slayer's blood isn't the same. You've been

augmented to be stronger, faster, more perceptive. To be sensitive to things a normal human would never see. But you shouldn't be able to do things like peel back the veil and see beyond, even if these abilities are given as a gift."

I stared at him. The implication in his words was obvious at this point, and yet I couldn't wrap my head around what he was saying.

"I'm not human?" I said finally. The question hung in the air, surreal.

"You can't be," Logan answered. "It's impossible." He paused thoughtfully, then amended his statement. "That is, you can't be *fully* human. Maybe you're half, or a quarter. But you aren't mostly human, either."

I was stone silent for at least a minute, dumbfounded, my mind racing, thinking of the vampire bite I survived when I was younger. How that was impossible, and yet here I was, still alive. I couldn't explain that or my strength for so long, so was this the reason? Then I let out a bewildered laugh. "What the fuck. How are you so sure about that?"

Just as patiently as before, Logan said, "I told you. The fact that you can accept any aspect of my power, let alone all of it, is irrefutable proof. A true mortal would either see nothing, or they would become overwhelmed and expire."

"Did you learn that from experience?" I had meant it as a lighthearted joke, but his answer didn't match my tone.

"Yes." He glanced away.

Instant guilt flooded in. "I'm sorry. You're right. You have to be right, I guess." The next question popped immediately into my head, and although I felt like a dumbass sending it out into the world, it had to be asked. "But if I'm not human, what the hell am I?"

"That I don't know yet."

I smiled internally. Of course that would be the one answer he didn't have. My head was still spinning, but I decided to have some fun with it. "What would you say if someone asked you? You've gotta have some idea."

He was quiet for a while, mulling it over. The hand working its way over and over through my hair paused in its tracks, so I held it. His fingers were long and slender, skin flawless and pale. Blue veins laced the underside of his wrist. *Like a living sculpture,* I mused. Just watching him exist was witnessing art in motion.

"A celestial being," he said at long last, nodding slightly. "Perhaps an angel."

I gazed up at his perfect features, long eyelashes shading those ice-blue eyes. "Like you."

Logan smiled. "No. Not like me at all."

I couldn't have related the events that followed in any kind of detail. I leaned up and kissed him again, and everything after that was a whirlwind of clothes coming off, skin on skin, waves of intense, long-anticipated pleasure. The next thing I knew, I was on my back, head flung backward, gripping the back of Logan's neck as he licked me until I wanted to scream. But not even the throes of impending orgasm could make me forget whose house we were in, nor who was upstairs at that very instant.

"Oh, fuck," I moaned. He leaned into me. My toes curled against the cushion. "Holy shit."

Logan tugged gently, easing away. "I'm sure you don't feel lucky at present, but you are." He ran his fingers down the soft skin on the inside of my thigh, leaving me trembling. "We don't have the same experiences that mortals do."

I opened my eyes. "Why not? You're missing out." I was at once intrigued and frustrated by his little aside. Leave it to Logan to drop knowledge as he edged me closer to the most intense climax of my life. The gradual buildup made it almost impossible to concentrate, despite my efforts. I really did want to know what he was going to say.

He licked his fingers, and when he put them

inside me, my eyes rolled back into my head, and my brain filled with erotic sensation. Before I could stop it, a guttural groan escaped from deep down in my chest. He pushed in and out of me as he rubbed my clit with his thumb.

I moaned louder, my hips bucking as he never paused. To say I lost my mind was a rather accurate picture as I writhed against his touch, desire roaring within me. My heart thumped louder, and there was no way I was turning back now.

"I suppose it's a necessary benefit for them." His hand started to make slow, deft strokes. I squeezed it impatiently, needing him to go back to what he was doing before. "They're going to die, so it's only fair that they can find solace in pleasure."

My whole body trembled. "I appreciate what you're saying, but I cannot have this conversation with you right now," I told him with urgency. "I need you to make me fucking come."

Logan grinned and fingered me faster once more until I couldn't stand the agony of being right on the edge anymore. In response to my desperate, mostly wordless pleas, he pulled me on top of him with ease. The moment I felt him push into me, I almost shrieked with pleasure. He was huge and hard, and all mine. He covered my mouth with his, stealing my cries of pleasure.

"Fuck me like this all the time," I whispered into his lips. "Oh, fuck, I need it so bad."

His thrusts were smooth and powerful, practically lifting me off the couch with every motion. I arched my back and wrapped my shaking legs around his waist. Every pleasure center in my brain exploded with him inside me. He seemed to know exactly how I needed him to touch me.

Sweat glistened across his brow, a deep rumbling roared in his chest as his fingers dug into my hips as he thrust into me each time I rocked down on him. Lust dilated his pupils, and I loved seeing the hunger behind them. Logan was always the calm one who rarely showed emotions, so to have him succumb from being with me did things to me. It made me adore him more. I have no idea how things had escalated so far with these three men. Monsters I would have called them once upon a time, but that was before they'd crawled under my breastbone and found a place in my heart. I didn't want to think about such emotions. I couldn't when my life was just too complicated.

Logan groaned, driving deep inside me, each thrust edging me closer and closer to my climax.

Then it hit hard and fast.

The orgasm crashed over me like a tsunami when it finally arrived. I gasped incoherently, trying to keep from raising my voice. All thoughts exited, replaced by physical sensation. I kept coming for what felt like an eternity—a journey of sheer ecstasy. Logan growled, reaching his own high, both of us tangled together and breathless.

Afterward, I ached with satisfaction and collapsed against him He kissed me softly, wrapping me in his arms. In the fog of the afterglow, I also wondered how long he'd been holding out on me. *None* of them had ever fucked me like that before. I made a sleepy mental note to notify Orion and Seth that the bar had officially been raised.

"Thank you," I murmured, snuggling in close. "I needed that more than you'll ever know."

Logan kissed the top of my head. I felt him smile once more. "I know."

CHAPTER 23

LOGAN

I hadn't meant to fall asleep on the sofa in the den, but when I opened my eyes, the light had changed. Veronica lay on her side, facing away from me. She only shifted a little as I carefully slipped out from underneath her body and pulled a blanket up around her shoulders. Her long eyelashes fluttered, but she didn't wake.

I leaned down and kissed her forehead. Any other night, I would have been happy to stay until she woke up on her own, but no matter where I was in the house, or what I was doing, I could feel Dylan's presence as tangibly as if he was following me around. He had been under Seth's supervision for a number of hours at that point; it was time for a shift change. And considering the reprieve I'd just been granted, I was willing to take on the next watch.

The cellar doors opened onto total darkness. Descending the stairs, I could see only the glowing yellow of Seth's eyes at first, and then the seated outline of our captive. He was hunched forward, his neck bent so that I couldn't see his face. I glanced at Seth.

"Don't look at me," the demon said. "There's nothing wrong with him. Nothing new, anyway."

At that, Dylan started to laugh. We stood there and watched his shoulders shake. Finally, he pulled himself upright and stared at us. His eyes were bloodshot, ringed with dark circles. "You guys are fucking idiots," he declared, still chuckling. "There's something wrong with me? You think it's that simple?"

"I mean, yeah." Seth rolled his eyes. "Fuck this. I've dealt with his bullshit long enough. I'm out." He patted me on the shoulder as he brushed past. "Good luck, angel-boy. I'll cover for you if you kill him."

He went up the stairs and was gone into the encroaching night. The doors creaked shut. I took up the post Seth had just vacated, and Dylan watched me with a keen gaze. "You never answered my question," he pressed. "Do you think it's as simple as me being fucked up?" He maintained a cool, irreverent tone, but I sensed some genuine curiosity underneath. As if he feared we might be right about him after all.

I let him stew in his own thoughts for a while. No part of me really wanted to engage with him on any level. I had a pretty good idea of where he had come from and what state he was currently in, and I wasn't particularly eager to have any theories confirmed. Then again, it wasn't like either of us had anywhere else to be.

I sighed. "No, I don't think that." After a moment's pause, I continued. "The vamp shaman didn't make a mistake. He used an unpredictable element."

"Interesting," Dylan muttered. Again, he made it seem like he was brushing me off. But a new wariness had entered his gaze. I wondered how much he really knew about his own resurrection.

"He didn't tell you how you came back, did he?" I asked. "In fact, I bet he just told you he was the one who did it, and that you should be grateful, because he granted you a second chance out of the goodness of his heart." Dylan issued no reply, which I took as confirmation. Except, I suspected I understood better how his return happened and where the wendigo vanished to. That the energy bringing Dylan back to life was a combination of the very creature that took Veronica's life and what remained of Dylan in the afterlife. I made a deal with the wendigo to aid us against the Seattle enemy that would return, which I believe had come in the form of a slayer. Leaning back on the cold cellar wall, I turned my eyes to the ceiling and smiled a little. "You were a slayer once. Do you remember what a wendigo is?"

CHAPTER 24

SETH

She was sleeping where I assumed Logan had left her, wrapped up in a blanket, his energy coming off her in waves. Orion was nowhere in sight. I slipped down onto the couch beside her, and she opened those pretty eyes and smiled. Then she blinked.

"You're not the one I was expecting," she murmured. "Not complaining, though."

I kissed her on the mouth, long and deep. She purred against my lips. "Angel-boy came down to the cellar," I said. "He's on duty. I'm off. No idea where the other one is."

Suddenly Veronica frowned. She pulled back a bit, her hand braced on my chest. "Where's Dylan?"

I frowned back at her. "He's downstairs where

we chained him up, V. And he's not going anywhere, so don't even think about it."

"Right." She relaxed, although the dismay was evident on her face. "God, it's so stupid to still be worried about him after all this." She laughed in a way that sounded like it was mostly to keep from crying.

I touched her face. "Yeah, it is. Don't feel bad. It's a human thing." She laughed again, more genuinely, and I hesitated. It seemed almost cruel to talk to her about Dylan in any capacity; no matter what I said, her image of him would end up shattered. But it bothered me more to lie to her, even by omission. "You know, we actually had a conversation down there."

"Oh yeah?" V tried not to sound interested and failed. She avoided making eye contact, resting her cheek against my chest. "That's surprising. I wouldn't have thought you two had much in common."

"We don't. I just wanted to know what the hell he thought he was doing, coming back from the dead only to get wrapped up in this mess." I wanted to wait for V to say something so I could gauge her emotions—to the best of my limited ability. Pain was a new thing for me, and yet I was determined to learn something about compassion for her sake.

She took a long time to answer, and when she did, I nearly didn't hear it. "It was me," she whispered. "He did it for me." She glanced up at me, eyes bright with unshed tears. "That's why it was so damn easy for the shaman. All he had to do was promise Dylan a way back to me."

I couldn't say she was wrong, and once she realized she'd pretty much nailed it, Veronica buried her head in my chest and sobbed. The sorrow overtook her like a storm. She clung to me, trembling. I didn't have anything else to do but hold her tight.

"It's not your fault," I murmured as reassuringly as possible. "We all have exploitable flaws." *All right, maybe that wasn't quite necessary.* "I mean, you couldn't have stopped them."

V brushed the hair from her face. She sniffled, wiping the tear streaks away with the backs of her hands. "I know what you meant." She leaned up and nuzzled the side of my neck and jaw. "And I know you're right. It's just horrible to deal with that kind of guilt. To think he hasn't been resting this entire time because of me."

I took her face in my hands, wiping the last stray

tear with my thumb. "Listen, that's his problem, not yours. Sometimes the dead stay around even though the people they loved are trying to let them go. Half the time, that's how they end up in Hell. They won't cross over on their own 'cause they can't wrap things up, they get trapped in their own shitty negativity, and then boom. In Hell forever."

She regarded me closely. "Is that what happened to you?"

I laughed. "Me? Of course not. I never leave anything unfinished."

Veronica shifted into my lap. She straddled my hips, ran her fingers into my hair. "Prove it," she demanded.

Her appetite impressed me after such a heavy bout of raw emotion. Maybe physical pleasure was cleansing for her, a way to release all the bad stuff. It was definitely a coping mechanism I could get behind.

She kissed my neck. I felt the edge of her tongue, and the barest hint of her teeth on my skin. Instantly, a fire ignited in my loins. The woman was nothing if not persuasive. And I didn't need to be told twice.

CHAPTER 25

ORION

The fact that Seth managed to get out of the cellar and see Veronica before I got back did not escape my notice. He wasn't there when I returned to the den, but her flushed skin and sensual aura told me everything I needed to know. Before, my instinctual reaction would have been an explosion of jealous rage, and I could not deny the urge to indulge in such anger. This time, however, something cautioned me to react in moderation. She had been satisfied, and she was happier than she had been. Wasn't that the least of what Veronica deserved?

"Hi." She reached a hand out toward me. The moment I touched her, I knew I'd gravely misunderstood her true emotional state. Perhaps the others had helped her release some tension, but she was not healed. Her eyes held worlds of sadness and confusion. I wondered if she had allowed them to see so deeply into her pain.

"Come on," I said gently. "Let's take a walk." She needed to get up and away from the place in which her past continued to fester underground. If I had my way, I wouldn't have let her return until the boy was removed from the premises. But of course, stubborn Veronica had her own ideas.

"Now?" She looked toward the window. "It's dark, Orion." She paused. "And…I know Dylan is still in the basement. I don't want to leave him." As if she was anticipating an unfavorable response, she added quickly, "Don't judge me. This has been hard enough already."

"I wasn't going to say anything," I half lied. "We won't go far. I think you could use the air." What I didn't say was that she seemed as though she'd been made from paper and eggshells—fragile, cracked, in imminent danger of collapse. I feared that the natural consequences of a slayer's decision to consort with her would-be prey were starting to catch up with her.

Veronica inhaled deeply and blew out her breath. "Maybe you're right," she finally conceded. She let me take her hand and pull her off the couch. Her fingers were cool to the touch. "I guess

I'm just…" She trailed off. I waited, as I was gradually learning how to do. "I'm uncomfortable. Nothing's felt good for days."

Unable to help myself, I raised an eyebrow. "Nothing?"

Veronica cracked a smile. "That's none of your business," she said. "I've been taken care of, thank you very much."

"Not by me." I led her out onto the porch and down the steps, being careful to guide her as far from the cellar entry as possible. Her gaze still flicked uneasily to the doors, which were barely visible along the side of the house.

"This is a stupid question," Veronica said slowly, "but do you think he'll be okay?"

I tightened my grip on her hand. "He's not going anywhere."

She shook her head. "I mean after this is over." When I didn't respond, she gave me a look. "Come on, Orion. I'm not stupid. I know you weren't planning to keep him in your basement forever. And I *know* you'd never let his ass into the clan."

"At least you give me that much credit," I muttered. "But really, I don't know what will happen to him." I hesitated. Part of me wanted nothing more than to force some sense into her, even if the task required some harsh language. She was too exceptional a woman to be so prone to damaging emotional attachments. It was obvious to everyone else that the boy she'd brought back from the other side of the veil was an abomination. The fact that she refused his true nature frustrated me to no end.

And yet, I didn't want to inform her of my plans to utilize him for the clan's benefit in the impending clash with Seattle. We'd already gone through one potentially relationship-altering fight; I knew better than to purposely start another. As I rose slowly from the ashes of my clan, Veronica stood as a beacon in sudden darkness, the only light I welcomed. Now she needed me as much as I needed her, if not more. My duty and my desire was to be there.

She frowned, furrowing her brow. "It feels horrible to think this after what we've all been through…but I keep thinking I made a mistake when I let Dylan follow me back into this realm." Veronica tucked a strand of hair behind her ear. "At first I was so excited—and I'm sorry if that hurt you, by the way. It was like I forgot all about everything I already had."

I chose not to reinforce how badly her choices had affected me. "I won't pretend I fully understand," I said. "But I forgive you."

She continued quietly. "Maybe it was the grief that got to me. Maybe I never really got over it, despite how hard I tried. His death was so sudden. So tragic. So violent." A shudder ran through Veronica's body. "I still have nightmares about it sometimes. I thought that having him back was everything I ever wanted." A mirthless laugh escaped her lips. "I should've known better."

Yes, you should have. I bit my tongue hard. Rarely did Veronica allow herself to display this kind of vulnerability; in fact, her toughness was one of the things I adored the most. It was strange and uncomfortable to see her open up this deeply. I could wound her in this moment, if I so chose. We both seemed to acknowledge that. Instead, I squeezed her hand. She squeezed back, hard.

"So stupid," she whispered. "Like, of course he was going to be changed. He was marinating in fucking purgatory for so damn long." Abruptly, she stopped and turned to face me, taking my other hand in hers. The way she stared into my face was broken and desperate. "Did I keep him there? God, tell me I didn't."

Admittedly, I was the exact wrong person to ask, and I wondered briefly why she hadn't saved the question for Seth or Logan. Then it occurred to me that perhaps she had asked them as well and been unsatisfied, or unsettled, by their answers. At some point in the past few days, Veronica had morphed into a haunted soul, dogged mercilessly by demons she had set upon herself.

I took her beautiful face into my hands. She wrapped her arms around my neck, pulling close for comfort. "You didn't keep him," I said. "He stayed. That's his fault, not yours." I paused for emphasis. "Do you understand, Veronica? None of this is your fault." She closed her eyes, releasing a shaky breath. I pressed my lips to her forehead. "If you want someone to blame, I'll volunteer," I added.

Her eyes snapped open again. "What?" Our embrace loosened. A frigid wind cut between us.

"That night when I saw you for the first time on the street, I chose you," I told her. "I wanted you, and I knew that you would be mine. One way or another."

The apprehension eased out of her features. "Well, I knew that." This time, her laugh was much more natural. "You weren't very subtle about it." One slender finger traced across my lips. "But I'm not granting that particular wish in full."

I attempted not to grimace and failed. "That's… fine." Not long ago, those two words would have comprised a complete lie. As it was, they made up maybe half a truth. I'd already determined that nothing would stop me from keeping Veronica, including whatever unconventional arrangement she demanded. There would be time for negotiations later, once the clan no longer stood on the very cusp of oblivion.

"Is it?" Veronica's tired gaze sparkled with a hint of mischief. The phantom of a heart swelled in my chest. I ached for her to be free from the shadows plaguing her life, and I knew I would do anything to make it so.

"Yes." I nodded as convincingly as possible. "I can always kill Seth if need be."

"I don't know about that." She smiled and stepped back, prompting our walk to resume. "He's pretty strong. And so is Logan."

"Who's your favorite?" I pretended her answer didn't matter, that I was just asking because she'd brought us all up together. "You must have one."

"Come on." Her tone turned vaguely reproachful. "You're all wildly different, and exciting, and sexy. I honestly never imagined I'd be able to find anything like what I have with each of you." She grew silent for a minute. "There's something about…us…that Dylan never gave me. I think that's why I'm able to consider life without him."

"You've been living life without him," I

reminded her. She winced a bit. I regretted the bluntness of my words.

"Yes." Veronica shook her head. "But I think this whole time I've been hoping deep down that he would miraculously show back up. And then he did, and it was too good to be true." Her voice broke. "The Dylan in my head is perfect. He was the love of my life for so long. I don't know how to say goodbye to him for good."

The conversation had brought us down to the shore of the inlet, where we stood side by side on the bank and looked out across the dark water. Veronica sniffled, wiping tears off her cheeks. I slipped my arm around her. She leaned into me.

"He isn't giving you a choice anymore," I said. "Either you let him go, or you go with him." I could feel her watching me closely.

"I can't," Veronica murmured. "I can't go with him."

"I know," I said. "Because we would never let you. We would follow you to the ends of the earth, to the furthest corners of time and space. There is nothing that could spare him from our wrath."

Veronica snuggled into my chest. I sensed her smile, although her face was hidden. "I'm not afraid of you, Orion," she said softly.

I kissed the crown of her head. When she was

in my arms like that, each beat of her pulse echoed through my body, the blood warm in her veins. The small, primal voice at the back of my mind commanded me to tilt her head to the side and claim her once and for all. The thought of my teeth sinking into her tender neck threatened to consume my consciousness.

But I forced the beast to stay dormant. The fangs in my mouth barely managed not to burst forth. I did not succumb to the raging tide of bloodlust.

"You don't need to fear me," I said to Veronica. "I don't want you to."

As we headed back up from the shore of the inlet, a shift in the air alerted all of my senses. A heavy, bitter current of energy had broken through from the south—the unmistakable warning of a storm on the horizon.

"Orion?" Veronica touched my face. "Are you okay?"

I glanced at her. "We're running out of time."

CHAPTER 26

VERONICA

I was tired. No, not just tired—exhausted. The kind of fatigue that creeps down into the bones and grows roots, like a weed. Every part of me ached: my body, my soul, my mind. I had a million thoughts and no way to sort them out. The only real reprieve I could find was in mindless pleasure, and so even though I was worn the hell out, I clung to Orion fiercely as he claimed me, plunging into me. He was fast, passionate, and a little rough, and this time I was happy to let him have his way. I craved the pain, the pleasure, all of it to forget the rest of my deranged messed up life.

Orion's lips slid over my whole upper body, lingering on my neck and on the crown of each breast. He devoured me more gently than usual, but his vampiric hunger still permeated every touch, every stroke, every thrust. I choked on the moans that came out of my mouth.

"Oh, God." My hands clenched around the edge of his bed, which I pretended did not also double as a dirt-filled vessel during the day. *This is crazy, Veronica,* my conscience whispered in between jolts of pleasure. *Is this really the path you're going to choose?* Before I had the chance to dwell on any of my doubts, Orion found a spot, deep between my thighs that made me roll my eyes back and bite the inside of my cheek.

My emotions might have been all ruined, but on the physical front, he had Dylan beat. I felt my knees start to buckle as my third breathtakingly intense orgasm of the day built to its peak. Orion's grip tightened on my hips and stomach. Suddenly, his smooth gyrations became frenzied. I clapped my hand over my mouth to keep from crying out. Stars danced in front of my eyes. I thought I might faint.

"Holy shit!" I collapsed back onto the bed, inhaling its cool, earthy smell. Orion stayed deep inside me as I squeezed around him, my body convulsing with the aftershocks. But then, as abruptly as he'd driven us both to climax, he pulled away. I glanced over to him. "What's up?"

The look on his face was so jarring that it snapped me back from a state of hazy euphoria. I turned over on the bedspread, fighting an onslaught of dread.

"They're on their way," he declared solemnly. "Right now." Seemingly without missing a beat, he had started to put his clothes back on. "We have to get the others and go." And just like that, playtime was over. I nodded and pushed myself to my feet. Orion tossed me the same clothes I'd been wearing for the last three days.

I guess this is what I'm wearing to war, I thought offhandedly. Of course, I had known since they left that it was only a matter of time before the Seattle clan came back again. They were the vamps on my home turf—I liked to think I was at least as familiar with them as Orion, if not more. Stubborn sons of bitches, persistent as hell. And they absolutely hated to lose by any measure.

"Who do we have coming to back us up?" I asked as we moved out into the hallway.

"Trent." Orion looked uncomfortable calling Trent by name, but I was proud of him for doing it. "And whoever he has seen fit to bring." He gestured toward my pocket. "Call him. Let him know the timer has run down."

"I'm on it." I had the phone up to my ear on the way down from the third floor. My mind scrambled for the right combination of words to say. *Get over here, loser. We're going to fight the bad guys.*

Trent answered almost instantly. I could tell from his voice and the background noise that he was moving, and probably pretty fast. "We're almost there," he said. "Don't worry."

"Tell me you brought a goddamn army," I answered. "I have a feeling we're going to need one." In fact, the closer I got to the outside of the house, the stronger I sensed the disturbance that had caught Orion's attention. By the time we stood in the yard, it was practically suffocating. No wonder Trent hadn't needed me to call.

"I got everyone who would come on less than a day's notice," he told me now. It was not the kind of reply that sparked confidence.

"Where would you put our chances, if you had to guess? Assuming Orion and company are fighting on our side."

"Right." He paused for longer than I liked. "I think it will be enough."

The apprehension gnawing at my gut only

intensified. "I hope so." It was my turn to hesitate. "Lian isn't with you, is she?"

"No, V. She's safe at home, although she's worried sick. You can come see her when this is all over."

I pressed my lips together. "If she can even bring herself to look at me." Never in my life had I felt like a worse friend, or a bigger piece of shit. How could I begin to make up for the staggering idiocy I had displayed over the past few weeks? Lian had called me for help, and what did I do? I came to Anchorage and fucked the local clanmaster. *Great job, V. I'm sure that's exactly what she had in mind.*

"Hey V, snap out of it." Trent's voice yanked me back into the present moment. "I need you to tell Orion that we're going to try to divert them away from the city—minimize collateral damage and all that. Meet us on the outskirts of Chugach, all right? The trees will give us some extra cover. Maybe we can use it to our advantage."

I already knew Orion wouldn't appreciate the change of venue. As far as I was aware, he hadn't stepped foot within park boundaries since the massacre in the grove. But Trent's thinking was logically sound. We needed all the advantages we could get, and if the city could also be spared the brunt of any potential damage, that was just bonus icing on the cake.

"I'll let him know," I said. "See you soon."

Orion stood frozen in the middle of the yard, eyes fixed on the slate-grey sky. His aura flared, absorbing energy from as far a distance as he could manage. The expression on his face had turned into a stony mask. When he heard me approach, his gaze flicked to the side, posture unchanged.

"What news?" he asked. *It better be good,* was the clear subtext of the question.

I arched my eyebrows. "Trent said they're drawing the Seattle contingent southeast, away from the city." He got my meaning before I mentioned the destination by name, but I did it anyway. "Toward Chugach. We need the cover of the woods."

Orion's sharp golden eyes narrowed dangerously. "The ground there is sacred to my clan," he growled. "Steele and his men wouldn't dare tread upon it."

I looked him directly in the face. "You and I both know damn well they would. And they will." I reached for his hand, turning east. "Let's go, Orion. Let Logan and Seth know that's where we'll be." The moment the words passed my lips, I froze for a split second, remembering that one or both of them had to be down in the cellar with Dylan at that very moment. A cold chill ran through me. I glanced at Orion again. Some of the bravado exited my voice. "What are we going to do about… him?" I nodded in the direction of the cellar doors.

Orion's face darkened. He glared sullenly at the cellar himself, and I knew he was consulting with the others, most likely excluding me on purpose. A little petty from my perspective, but at the same time, I couldn't really blame him anymore. My track record for acting rationally in Dylan's presence was pretty dismal, at best. A few tense moments passed. I wondered if Orion might risk leaving one of the boys behind—or, more importantly, if either Seth or Logan would allow it.

It turned out to be a moot point. "We have to bring him with us," Orion announced, in a way that made his displeasure very evident. He marched ahead. "They will escort him. You and I are proceeding on ahead."

The stupid, delusional, lovesick part of my brain, the part that still wanted to believe I could find a way to keep Dylan in my life without doing irreparable harm, urged me to stay behind and join the escort. I shoved it down and caught up to Orion in a burst of speed. For once, the correct choice was obvious. *You can do this, V,* I coached myself, as the house fell farther and farther away. *You can let go.*

But there was something else that slowed me down on the way out of Anchorage. Not Dylan, but a different voice slipping inconspicuously in between my thoughts. I recognized Logan's unfailingly serene energy right away.

Veronica. Wait for me in the forest. I need to speak with you. As usual, he gave no hints toward his intentions, good or bad.

"Oh, what the hell," I muttered under my breath. Apparently not even the threat of imminent battle was enough to keep a fallen angel from being weird and cryptic. Orion gave me a questioning look, but he was preoccupied, and when I said, "Nothing," he simply focused his eyes forward. I was grateful not to be pressed for details, and yet, Logan's comments needled at me the whole way out. Was he planning something? Did he have doubts, or maybe suspicions? Had he discovered some earthshattering information he didn't want Orion to hear?

Every possibility I thought of made my stomach ball up into knots. I wanted to turn around and haul ass back to the house, just to demand an immediate explanation. But we were hurtling along toward the northern boundary of the park, and if I stopped for any reason at this point, Orion's burning fuse might just explode.

There was nothing to do but wait and wonder. And hope against hope that no more terrible secrets were about to emerge from the dark.

CHAPTER 27

LOGAN

"They're here, aren't they?"

I could hear the sardonic smirk in Dylan's voice without looking at him. He walked behind me with his wrists tied in front. Seth was bringing him behind us.

"Don't try anything funny," the demon warned. "There's not much I'd like more right now than to beat the shit out of you." He spoke lightly, but each word carried an edge. His irritation was up, the hot blood in his veins creeping toward its boiling point. He, too, felt the electricity in the atmosphere.

"Maybe you should," Dylan chuckled coldly. "It might be good for both of us." Like Seth, he put up a nonchalant front that didn't quite mask the restless energy roiling beneath the surface. A multitude of mixed emotions colored his aura. I counted excitement, anger, resignation, and fear.

"Nah." Seth nudged the captive forward into the heavily overcast daylight. "I think you'd like it too much." He dropped the cellar doors shut with a resounding slam. "Just shut up and get moving."

Both Seth and I had received the message regarding the meeting point at Chugach. Dylan didn't comment as we steered him in that direction, though I wouldn't have been surprised if he knew exactly where we were headed. No telling how closely he was connected with the enemy.

During the journey to the park, I had the merciful luxury of flying high above and slightly ahead of Seth and Dylan. In theory, I was acting as a scout, in case the Seattle vamps had thought to try and catch us off guard. Mostly, however, I was just glad to get away from the dark cloud of tension enveloping all three of us. Seth had not exaggerated his level of animosity.

From my vantage point high in the murky gray sky, I could glance down and see the two of them making their way across the Alaskan terrain. Seth matched every move that Dylan made to a fearsomely precise degree. He was prepared to strike at any time, and I had little doubt he'd even think twice about dealing a killing blow. In many ways, it must have been easier to rationalize killing Dylan and answering to Orion for his recklessness than enduring another moment in the company of such an unpleasant individual.

I kept an eye on them at all times, half expecting to see Dylan's body collapse amid a scarlet arc of blood. Seth's temper was palpable, his volatile energy sizzling more ferociously the nearer we came to battle. I wondered how long he'd be able to keep himself in check, as well as how I might help him explain Dylan's smoking, eviscerated corpse.

But I knew the route to Chugach well now, and my mind was occupied by other, even more pressing matters. Veronica's identity—her true one, as defined by the kernel of magic nestled deep within her spirit, was a puzzle I'd been trying to solve for hours. I had been in casual denial for much too long—and for what reason? Perhaps the idea of adding yet more intrigue to an already complex situation was too exhausting to even consider.

Or maybe I had simply come to enjoy the way things were. As I knew her currently, Veronica was easy to admire and easy to understand. She was strong but mortal; her brief and tempestuous life little more than a ripple in the river of time. Their brevity was one of my favorite things about humans; it kept me from too much effort in the same way it kept me from pain.

If I was correct in my new assumptions about her, everything had changed. The scope of her future could be huge. Even a young celestial being had the right to laugh in the face of death. It occurred to me that she'd already done it at least once. Maybe more than that. I needed to talk to her.

Halfway to Chugach, heavy raindrops began to fall. They rolled off the tips of my feathers, plummeting like stones toward the landscape racing by below.

This is fucking bullshit, Seth growled somewhere underneath me.

Speed up, I told him. *Don't let them gain an advantage.* I leaned into my flight, beating my wings a little harder. The rain soaked my face and hair. It almost felt cleansing, in a strange way. A purification before the commencement of battle.

Oh, don't worry, Seth replied. *I did not come this far to lose to a pack of street rats.* The scowl was audible in his voice.

I shifted my attention forward, toward our destination. The rain had not deterred the oncoming forces—they pressed on in much the same manner as us, coming up from the south to clash at the border of the park. My window of opportunity to speak with Veronica was narrowing rapidly.

I'm going ahead, I told Seth. Without waiting for an answer, I bore down on my wings until the wind ripped by. My shoulders ached, but it didn't matter. The conversation I wanted to have could not wait until after the fight was over; in fact, the outcome might depend on it.

No problem, Seth barked back. *Don't bother warning me or anything. I'm sure we'll be fine.* He paused. *Actually, that gives me an excuse to whip this kid's ass into shape. Go as fast as you want.*

I had already left them in the distance. The voice of the wind had risen to a roar, drowning out all other sounds except my own thoughts. My worst fear was that the Seattle clan knew or had learned as much about Veronica as I thought I knew, and that they had beaten me to the punch in terms of creating a plan to deal with her.

There was a very good chance that she was in immediate danger. I wanted to tell Orion to protect her extra vigilantly, but his natural flair for the dramatic risked costing us time we didn't have. Instead of warning him, I resorted to pushing my body to its absolute limit in terms of strength and speed. The rain had turned to a thin coat of ice on my skin. Every color melted into a raging blur.

Then I spotted two figures half a mile from Chugach's edge. They were moving fast like me, flashes of deep black and the telltale pink of Veronica's hair. I angled down to swoop low over them, heading straight for the dense tree line. Veronica turned her face up as I passed, her eyes wide but knowing.

The landing I made carved a trough in the dirt ten feet long, and I ended with my body braced against the dark trunk of a tree that would have been happy to smash me to pieces. The world came back into focus.

"Logan!"

I turned around. A cloud of feathers, loosened by the wild flight, burst from my wings. Veronica ran toward me, concern etched on her face. She skidded to a halt beside my tracks.

I touched her face. "Hello. Walk with me for a minute."

She frowned. "What's wrong? You scared the shit out of me, coming in like a bat out of hell. Are you okay?" Her hands began to wander over me, searching for any signs of injury. Gently, I brushed her off.

"There's not a lot of time. They'll arrive very

soon." I grabbed her by the hand, aware that Orion was coming up along Veronica's side. His eyes bored into me, burning with unasked questions. I paused just long enough to give him a meaningful stare. "Seth and the other one are on their way."

Orion didn't appear to fully understand what I was doing, and he didn't like it either. But he nodded, tight-lipped, and let me pull Veronica away without pursuing. I led her deeper among the trees.

"Logan..." she said again, her tone becoming vaguely wary. "What is this about?"

"Were you supposed to survive on the day that Dylan died?" The question was purposefully abrupt so that she was more likely to be honest in her surprise.

"I—" She stopped. "I don't know." The wariness in her gaze increased tenfold. "My memory of everything except his death is patchy."

"Did you get hurt?" My thoughts backpedaled to the most recent time I had seen her naked—was there any evidence of old wounds? Wounds that should have been fatal?

Veronica rubbed her jaw. Her eyes went hazy as she dove into the rawest, most painful part of her past. Suddenly, a spark of clarity kindled in her expression. She looked startled. "I think I might have. I remember Lian telling me she had to throw away the clothes I was wearing because of the blood. And I assumed she meant Dylan's blood, but she made a comment about how not all of it was his."

"You *were* injured." I ran a palm over the contours of her torso. "Where?"

"That's the weird thing," she said quietly. "I have no idea. If there was an injury, I don't recall it. Like, at all. I was devastated for weeks, but I wasn't hurt." Veronica took a step toward me. "Tell me what you're getting at. We're short on time, remember?"

"I don't think you're simply mortal." The words came out fast, because she was right, and anything other than pure directness would have been wasting seconds. "It's like I said before. You shouldn't be able to use my power. You shouldn't be able to bridge between realms. Those things aren't learned in the way a slayer's craft can be."

"You weren't joking, then." She gazed up at me. "Before we—"

I sighed. "Have I *ever* told you a joke? No, I wasn't joking. You are something more, and I believe we might need you to tap into that power very soon."

"What the hell!" Veronica threw up her hands.

"I barely have any idea what you're talking about, Logan. How am I supposed to use this alleged power?"

"Let's see if this helps." I took her face in my hands and kissed her hard on her beautiful mouth. She grabbed my arms as a sudden wave of energy crashed through us both. The sensation was like that of a key unlocking, a practically tangible click.

We eased apart. "Listen," she said breathlessly. "I know we hooked up in the woods that first time, but I don't think—" Her eyes widened. Then they started to glow. "Wait. Whoa."

I smiled. "There it is."

Veronica drew in a deep, slow breath. "I can see…everything," she whispered. Her eyes roamed the surroundings. "Every shred of life. Every scrap of energy." She paused, facing south. "The Seattle clan is a mile away. There's a shitload of them."

"We're outnumbered?" I asked, though I knew the answer.

"Yeah." She chewed her lip. "Extremely."

I nodded. "That's why we needed to talk. You have to be operating at full capacity for us to have a fighting chance."

"Holy shit." She looked down at her hands and back at me. "Am I supposed to be giving off light?"

"Never seen a celestial who didn't," I answered.

The look she was giving me turned searching. "You must have been like this once too, weren't you?" she asked. "That's how you knew. And how you were able to awaken me just now, but Orion and Seth never did."

"A demon and a vampire aren't going to possess the keys to celestial power." I glanced away. "And… I suppose you're right. At some point, I may have been…" I gestured indistinctly at her. "But none of that matters after an angel falls."

Veronica touched my shoulder. "Will you tell me that story someday?"

"Not right now," I said. "We're wasting time."

She rolled her eyes. "That's why I said *someday*. Also, you get to explain this to Orion if he asks."

"He probably won't," I said. "Yet."

Orion didn't ask. But he was waiting impatiently on the edge of the thick woods where we reemerged. Instantly, he homed in on the difference in Veronica's aura, and I thought he might forgo the questions entirely in favor of fighting me on the spot. How he despised to be left out of anything, especially relating to her!

"Where's Seth?" Veronica asked, partially to defuse the influx of tension. She looked around again. "And…"

As if on cue, I heard the demon's voice.

If you want this son of a bitch alive, come take him off my hands. Fucker's trying to go rogue.

"Oh, shit," Veronica muttered. She bolted toward Seth's presence. Orion and I followed in her wake.

CHAPTER 28

SETH

I could almost respect the time it had taken for the kid to do something incredibly stupid—that is, beyond the myriad ways in which he'd already fucked up. His stint in the cellar was remarkably peaceful; I had to admit that he had really tried to play nice. A few snide comments were nothing I couldn't handle.

But I had sensed him getting ready to rebel from the moment his Seattle buddies entered the scene. Their encroaching presence alone activated him like a guided beacon. *Stop being so fucking docile,* I imagined them saying. *Act like an asshole. That's your job.*

Still, well within my handling capabilities. The bastard had proven to be tougher than he looked, but I was fully confident in my ability to put him down like a goddamn dog, should the need arise. Not even Logan taking off to fly ahead fazed me, although I'd had better company in worse places. By that time, I'd begun to notice that the darkness in his aura was welling up and oozing out, sitting on the surface of his energy like oil on water.

Great. Exactly the kind of shithead I want to be babysitting. Logan was barely a speck in the clouds. I could talk to him if I wanted, but Dylan and I were more or less alone. That was when he started to watch me. The same way a caged animal watches its keeper, waiting for the perfect opportunity to make a break for it.

"I know what you're thinking," I told him calmly, "and you'd better stop, or else you'll be a dead man walking."

The kid laughed. "Don't we both know I already am?"

I scoffed, unimpressed. If he had any illusions about the type of man he was dealing with, I was prepared to dispel them real quick. As far as I was concerned, Orion might still be able to strike a bargain with the other vamps using Dylan's fresh corpse. And if that didn't work, we'd figure something out. Working under pressure was kind of my specialty, as a demon from Hell.

That was why I didn't panic when I felt his

energy shift on approach to Chugach's boundary. No one needed to be there to tell me the little weasel was gonna try to cut and run. His intentions were clear as day—on his face, in his manner, in the way he subconsciously braced against the bindings on his wrists. He might as well have told me out loud that he was about to betray the unspoken agreement we had reached up to this point.

I was ready for it the instant he attempted to charge me and get away. He tucked in his arms and threw his shoulder forward. Maybe he thought the element of surprise was all he needed. It gave me immense satisfaction to know he was wrong.

The point of Dylan's shoulder struck my hands instead of my chest. I absorbed the impact and used his momentum against him, following his trajectory through in one swift push. His head snapped up in panicked realization a second too late; his balance had already passed the tipping point. I had the pleasure of standing back and watching him crash to the ground. Without his arms free to catch him, he hit hard.

"Dammit!" He slithered around to face me, pulling his legs up to shield his vulnerable stomach. I could've taken the opportunity to crush his balls or step on his throat, two options that both appealed to me. But then the amount of time I had spent suffering in his presence would amount to little more than an empty, annoying waste.

"That all you got?" I smirked. "Pretty weak. Get your ass up, and let's go. People are waiting on us." I chose not to give him a hand—it was much more satisfying to watch him struggle to his feet.

He spat at me. "Fuck off. It was worth a shot." I started to turn away, thinking we might actually make the remaining quarter mile without too much drama. Then I saw him out of the corner of my eye, flat-out making a run for it.

Maybe I should have held on to him after all. I frowned and took off in pursuit, bursting up to maximum speed. Smoke rose from the ground under my feet; each footstep left behind a charred print. I was gaining on him right away, but not as quickly as I expected, which was disturbing. What kind of deep sorcery had been pumped into him?

We tore a path parallel to the looming tree line. Every few seconds, the fugitive would toss a glance over his shoulder, as if he actually thought I'd let his sorry ass get away. He deserved a little bit of credit for forcing me to break a sweat, but his hobbled wrists messed with his equilibrium. One foot caught in a hole in the dirt, and he was sent stumbling. Even though he managed not to fall, the misstep slowed him down enough that I was able to land a flying tackle. I thought I felt something snap beneath my weight. The kid grunted.

"Next time, you're dead," I told him calmly. "I won't even chase."

He didn't waste a drop of energy on a reply. His whole body lurched as he tried to throw a punch in the general direction of my face. Once again, I was surprised by the measure of his strength. Unfortunately for him, it wasn't enough anymore.

"Are you kidding me?" I'd been doing my best not to inflict unnecessary violence or damage him any further, because I was certain it wasn't what Veronica would want. Now her little ex-boyfriend was wearing my limited patience thin. I took a deep breath and sent out a call to Logan and Orion. Not for help, per se—just to let them know the situation. He needed to become someone else's problem fast.

Dylan squirmed again, attempting to grab at me. One arm seemed dead, which pleased me and frustrated him to no end. He growled like a feral animal, his eyes full of black rage.

"I hope you fucking burn," he snarled. "You don't belong here, with her."

"That's funny," I said. "Neither do you."

CHAPTER 29

ORION

The scene I saw playing out three hundred yards from where we'd been standing was Seth pinning Dylan down, pressing the side of his face into the earth. Seth looked bored, his expression a stark contrast to Dylan's obvious, burning fury. Veronica broke ahead of Logan and me. I could see a faint trail of her energy shimmering in the air behind her.

"It's not what it looks like," Seth told her flatly as she reached them. "Well, okay, it kind of is. Lover boy wanted to bail, but I said no."

"He's not my lover," she responded without a trace of breathlessness. She knelt down to look Dylan in the eyes. "I'm sorry that you had to spend so many years in a terrible place. And I wish things had turned out differently."

"That makes two of us," Dylan said bitterly. Seth took the pressure off his head, and he sat up, shoving space between himself and the demon. "Get off me, you hellrat."

"Hey." Veronica glared at him. "Watch your mouth."

"Really?" He laughed and shook his head. "I can't believe you're defending him now instead of me. I was an idiot to think we could just pick up where we left off, or that you'd be the same girl I remembered." He scrutinized her. "It's a real fucking shame, V. Some might call it a waste."

She winced. "We both know I'm not the only one who's changed." Her voice was strong, but tight, the voice of a woman determined not to cry.

"You'd be nothing without your entourage."

I had heard enough. "Shut him up," I said to Seth. "Just grab his legs and drag him. They're close." For once, Seth was happy to oblige. He leaned over, seized Dylan by the ankles, and hauled him toward the trees. The captive put up some semblance of a fight, but his dragging right arm made all his efforts futile. I waited for Veronica as the others went ahead.

"I was going to ask what you're about to do with him," she said, rubbing her eye with the heel of her hand. "But then it would be even harder to convince myself I don't care anymore."

"Come on." I brushed her hair out of her face. "It's time to go."

At the edge of the woods, we stood watch, grouped around our prisoner like the actors in a sacrificial ritual. As shapes began appearing in the distance, moving toward us, I stepped away from the trees and into the open. Trent led the pack, and as he drew nearer, I realized he was running.

"Something's wrong." Veronica had come up behind me. She stared into the distance, brow furrowed, and then her expression suddenly changed. "Oh, fuck. They must have been ambushed." Over her shoulder, she called, "Let's go, you guys!" And with that, she was off, blazing a path straight toward our reinforcements.

Not wanting to be outdone, I stayed on her heels. She was wildly beautiful to me in those moments, permeating with a peculiar serenity, that we spent rushing to meet our reckoning. It met us in the form of a stampede of vampires, pale and ghastly in the overcast light, reeking of the grimy streets of Seattle.

The moment we were within striking distance, Trent swung around and bellowed to his fighters, "Turn!" Despite my skepticism that a human slayer was capable of holding a strong enough command, they turned as one, crashing back into the enemy like the angry tide.

The vampires shrieked, disappearing in a storm of teeth and claws. Almost immediately, I smelled blood misting in the air. Logan and Seth dove into the chaos. An enemy vampire, twisted with age and power, leapt toward my throat. I bared my teeth and ripped him out of the air.

His impact still knocked us both to the ground. I tore at him, feeling the snap of bone and the sickeningly satisfying tear of cloth and skin. He was cold to the touch, his true strength belied by the gaunt appearance of a desiccated corpse.

"You!" the elder vampire snarled, baring ancient, blackening fangs. Yellow eyes, sunk deep into shriveled sockets, still gleamed with the fire of deep-seated hatred. "You will never be worthy of the master's title." One bony palm dug into my chest. His fingers curled over until the nails had pierced my shirt and raked against the skin beneath. "There is no place for you at the head of a clan, and for your indiscretions, you shall pay!"

For the second time that day, I had heard enough. Whatever drivel Steele was feeding his clan had poisoned their minds, made them casualties of his blind pursuit of power. I grabbed the elder by his scraggly throat and flipped him over. He wheezed in pain, but his glare remained unrepentant.

"Where is Steele?" I demanded. "This fight is ours, old man. Not yours."

He coughed in between spurts of uneven laughter. "I would die before leading you to him."

"Very well." I drove my hand straight into the left side of his chest, pushing aside flesh and bone. The cruel light drained from his eyes as quickly as the flipping of a switch. It was, at best, an undignified way to end a life so long. *Truly,* I thought, with some measure of irony, *we are masters of our fate.*

When I stood up, my mind singularly focused on the search for Steele, my gaze fell upon a panorama of chaos. The only thing I could tell with any certainty at a glance was that there were far more of them than there were of us. A bitter smile curled my lip. Perhaps some diplomacy would have been a wise investment.

But it was too late for regrets. I pushed my way through the battle, fending off a constant barrage of attacks, keeping my head as far down as I could manage. That first encounter had shown me that being recognized here would only end in disaster. Some might have called it foolish to seek out

Steele alone, without protection. A reckless flirtation with death.

Nonetheless, I had no fear, only cold resolve. I had spoken the truth to the elder who now lay dead by my hand. This fight was between the two of us—no one else. And one way or another, it was going to end today.

CHAPTER 30

VERONICA

I did not like to admit it publicly, but as a slayer, I was always kind of into a good fight. There was just some adrenaline-powered, sick thrill in beating the hell out of what usually amounted to the boogeymen from everyone's childhood nightmares. This attitude had changed since arriving in Anchorage, for obvious reasons, and yet I still felt an incredible sense of catharsis in the middle of the fray.

Maybe it had something to do with the fact that most of my opponents didn't really bleed. Even as I charged at a big, barrel-chested vamp, used my staff as a vault, and catapulted backwards off his pecs, striking the vamp rushing up behind me on the way down, the violence seemed almost like a cartoon. I speared the second guy through the chest and threw him at the big vamp, who stumbled back into another of his friends.

It was some grisly shit, but the pounding beat of my heart and the blood rushing through my veins washed it all away. I had long since learned not to think on the job. Once the training kicked in, it was like riding a bike. A screeching, violent bike that was constantly trying to kill me.

"What are you doing here, bitch?"

I whipped around at the sneering voice and came face to face with a woman who could have been any of the others. Her thin, sallow face contorted in disgust at the sight of me, and I got the impression that I was supposed to recognize her in turn.

Instead, I frowned and asked, "Do we know each other?"

She sniffed. "Oh, everyone knows you. Thinking you're such hot shit with your pink hair. Like you don't even need to worry about staying hidden, right? Because you're just *that good.*"

I stared at her in utter confusion. "What the fuck are you talking about?" My grip tightened instinctively on the handle of my staff. I wondered how fast I could stake her if she tried to make a move. In just the last few minutes, I'd been getting plenty of practice, so I thought the odds were in my favor.

She rolled her eyes. "You make me sick. Frankly, I'm impressed you showed up here. I didn't think you had it in you, since you're so good at running away." In a flash, her hand darted toward me. "And if you ever think about setting foot back in the city, you're a dead girl walking."

I knocked her hand out of the air. She hissed, drawing it back, and then she dropped all pretense and just lunged at me. Shifting my weight to my back foot, I jabbed the end of the staff sharply upward, exactly where I judged she would be.

She never completed that ill-advised leap. Her body crumbled off the edge of the weapon. I kept it at the ready, glancing around. "Anyone else?"

That was when I noticed something strange going on. The frenzy of fighting all around me had subsided, almost as if some of the vamps had been called off. A feeling of dread spawned in my stomach, and I looked around again, scouring the battlefield for anything out of place. My intuition screamed that we were about to be in big trouble.

Then I saw the man, a hundred feet away, walking calmly through a parting sea of vampires. I watched brutal skirmishes pause as he went by, often to the disadvantage of the vampire choosing to show reverence. His presence seemed to over-ride the clamor of battle completely.

He was heading straight for me. It seemed like a terrible idea to move toward him, so I held my ground where I stood, staff at the ready. The closer he got, the more I sensed his aura permeating through the atmosphere. The magic brewing in his energy tugged at the corners of my mind.

Submit, it whispered. *It's not too late to join the winning side.*

I scowled. I caught his pale, powerful gaze. His expression betrayed no emotion whatsoever. Like Logan, but worse in a way I couldn't articulate.

"Fuck this," I said out loud. My voice carried unexpectedly; heads turned in my direction. The advancing figure gave no sign that he had heard me, although I was sure he did. He kept walking. It began to dawn on me that maybe I wasn't the one he cared about. As soon as he got in range, I stepped up to stop him myself. "I don't think I can let you go any farther."

He looked down at me. The top of his face was covered by a creepy mask of bone, pale white everywhere except for heavy black around the eyes. "I'm afraid you have no choice," he answered. Before I could react, he placed a hand over my face. I blinked, and when my eyes opened again, I was looking down at the top of my own head, a passive observer as my body crumpled to the ground. The man continued on his path as though nothing had happened.

"What the hell!" I shouted. My voice, which had carried so far only moments before, might as well have been muffled under ten pillows. Panic swelled in my chest. Was I dead? Was I unconscious? There was no way to know from there. Frantically, I kicked at the air—and to my surprise, I moved a little. Further experimentation showed that if I was careful, I could sort of swim back down toward my body. What happened after that, I didn't know, but it didn't matter.

I had seen where the figure was headed. He was going toward the thickest part of the trees, which was also the last place I'd seen Dylan.

Considering the circumstances, I couldn't call it a coincidence.

I clawed my way downward, full of determination and anger. *This is going to be the last walk you ever take, buddy. I fucking promise you.*

LOGAN

I had just finished off an enemy when I felt Veronica's spirit be pulled from her body. Instantly, all my senses were on high alert. I summoned my power in a desperate bid to call her back from wherever she was headed—but my calls were met with confusing silence. If she were truly dead, I should have seen her, should have been able to reach out and grab her. Instead, she was traveling away from me, on a trajectory at first parallel to the mortal realm, and then decidedly back toward it.

She didn't need me to rescue her from death again. She was doing it herself. An eerie calm began to spread over the scene of our endless fight. The signal of her spirit was slowly being diminished by a foreign energy, rare in its power. It made the hair stand up on the back of my neck; I knew that tranquility could be as bad an omen as any.

I pushed through the battlefield, tracking the path of Veronica's spirit. It wasn't long before I spotted her body. Even in all forms of death she was beautiful, as if she was merely resting. But the grim tableau didn't scare me as much as it might have if I couldn't also see her spirit struggling mightily to rejoin its vessel.

"Veronica!" I ran to where she lay and reached up to get her attention. Her spirit turned toward me, her expression a mix of surprise, relief, and delight.

"Oh, thank fuck you're here." She stretched an arm toward me. "I gotta go, or he's going to get away."

I grabbed her hand and pulled her earthward, using my body as an in-between to allow her to bridge the gap between the ether and the corporeal. She passed through me almost too quickly; the world spun for a moment or two. Then she sprang up off the ground.

"Who did this?" I asked. "I felt it happen."

"I don't know who he is," she said. "But I'm gonna fucking kill him." She turned to go, but quickly came back. "Hold on." Then she gave me a quick, passionate kiss. I sensed her drawing on my power just a little bit, enough to augment her own.

"Go get that son of a bitch," I said.

"I will." She winked.

That might have been the moment I truly fell in love.

CHAPTER 31

VERONICA

$\mathcal{I}$ had never run faster or harder than I did that day, with Logan on my lips. He was my invigorator, my bulwark in a storm, and his power seemed to dovetail with mine in a way I hadn't noticed before. The energy in the air became a map showing me every step that bastard had taken. In places, I could literally see his footsteps pressed into the ground. My stomach sank when I noticed that each stride was lengthening.

He was picking up the pace, and so I did too. The trees formed a dark wall looming high over me, and the shadows they cast were long and dark. But he was in there—the footprints told me so. I leaned into my sprint, urging my body forward. Then the soft muttering of a disembodied voice touched my ears.

I didn't know how to decipher the words; they belonged to a language beyond my understanding. The tone, however, and the malice behind it, I could definitely register. The incantation floated from behind a cluster of trunks just ahead.

Was this where we left Dylan?

As soon as I asked myself, I began to pick out the subtlest threads of Dylan's energy, flowing alongside the route I was already tracing. My sneaking suspicions had just been confirmed. This asshole had been after Dylan the whole time.

And now he was trying to put something unknown into action. The chanting intensified, both arms lifting from his sides. His hands began to glow, dimly at first, and then the light crept along his arms, into his shoulders, centering in the middle of his chest. He lifted his eyes to the sky, shifted position, and I glimpsed Dylan's form sitting upright against a tree trunk.

"Shit," I whispered. At first, Dylan seemed limp and unresponsive, and I didn't know whether to feel dread or relief. Then, without any kind of warning, he picked up his head, and the dial turned all the way to dread. Still wasn't sure what was going on, but I knew I couldn't just stand by and watch. My window to act was small and constantly shrinking.

I took a deep breath, filling my lungs with cool forest air. Logan's taste still simmered on my lips, his power in my soul. I called mine forth the same way I had called his, dipping into the well of strength on the other side of the veil. Where there had once been little more than a slow but steady stream, I now found a river feeding into a deep, clear pool.

Sudden searing pain ripped through my shoulders. I bit my lip hard to keep from gasping—or swearing. My shoulder blades jerked backwards, and I found myself awash in gleaming feathers drifting down from overhead.

"No way," I whispered. It was impossible to contain the wonder filling my heart. The wings were heavy, and they kind of hurt. I flexed those muscles and winced. But they beat strongly, almost on their own. My feet lifted off the ground. I focused all my attention on my target, whose own ethereal trance had made him oblivious.

At his feet, Dylan had started to struggle against his bonds. It was now or never. As I drew my staff, the striking end exploded into a brilliant, flaming blade. At the same time that I shot forward on the force of my wings, I swung the blade up and then brought it down in a smooth, remorseless arc.

At the last second, all trances were broken. The

man in the mask whipped his head around, but his reaction came a fraction of a second too late. I barely felt the blade cleave his body; all I saw was him falling to the ground. The blood pouring from the wound soaked the surrounding soil in tainted darkness. Faint trails of smoke ribboned up into the sky.

Soon, he'd be reduced to a pile of dust, and it would no longer matter who he was or what he did. At least, not to anyone who might come upon his remains before they were carried away on the wind. I was always glad to be rid of vamps so quickly, but it also annoyed me that winning a battle often meant losing all concrete evidence of their existence.

"You came back." Dylan grinned with one side of his mouth. He was dirty and disheveled now, and I could have sworn he looked paler. The dark circles under his eyes seemed to deepen every second.

"Was that him?" I asked. "Your benefactor?"

He nodded. "And you killed him without a second thought. Not sure how I feel about that—although I guess this new thing is pretty cool." Dylan gestured vaguely to the bright wings, the cascade of feathers. I couldn't tell if he was being sarcastic.

I rolled my eyes. "Stand up. I'm sorry we just left you here. Things got a little out of hand."

"You're right about that," Dylan said, "but you're not sorry."

"I am." I took him by the shoulder and helped pull him to his feet.

He turned to gaze at me, our faces inches apart. "How can you be sorry when you're about to walk me to the gallows?"

My heart clutched tight in my chest. Logically, I knew that I no longer had any obligation to care about what happened to Dylan at the hands of Orion, or any of the others. He had turned from the funny, confident, loving boy from my past to a bitter, hateful man so fast that I still had to process the emotional whiplash.

Nonetheless, I didn't quite have it in me to throw him to the wolves and look away. The idea that I would be the one to send him to his second death opened a yawning chasm of pain in my heart.

I let go of his arm and swallowed the lump in my throat. "Don't be so dramatic." I spoke with a false veneer of bravado. "I'm just not dumb enough to let you out of my sight again."

We stepped across the body of the slain shaman as the last of it moldered into the soil. Dylan glanced down at the ash seeping away into the dirt, but he said nothing. Part of me wanted desperately to know what he was thinking.

Part of me understood it didn't matter anymore.

CHAPTER 32

Negotiations were the most boring part of any war, as far as I was concerned. If it were up to me, I would have skipped straight to the part where I got to enjoy the spoils of victory—that is to say, V naked underneath me in bed, bursting with pleasure. Maybe she'd be tied to the bedposts or handcuffed to the headboard. Or maybe I'd leave her loose and let her fingernails draw tracks all over my body. After this shitstorm had finally passed, we'd have all the time in the world to figure out exactly how good we could make each other feel.

But first I had to stand at the edge of a dust-bathed forest and listen to a bunch of vamps fight over Veronica's ex. The good news was that the Seattleite bastards had backed off considerably following the death of their great shaman. I had looked up from my latest victory to see V strolling out of the woods with Dylan in front of her and two huge wings flowing from her shoulders. A pang of wild jealousy shot through me; it was infuriating, but not altogether surprising that angel-boy was the one she ended up matching. They had a special connection that even I, a lowly prince of Hell, could not deny.

The bad news? The only deal the Seattle clan was willing to strike meant that Dylan would go back to Washington with them, and therefore, we would not get to kill him ourselves. Physical vengeance against him had been a burning desire of mine practically from the instant I made his acquaintance, and the base, violent section of my brain resented the loss of that opportunity. But I also understood that V hadn't quite put out her torch for the little rat, whether anyone else agreed with her or not.

She wouldn't want to see him die, and she especially wouldn't want to see us kill him. That fact alone was enough to grant him grudging clemency. I could tell from the way he looked at her that Logan felt the same. As for Orion, no words had to be said. It was not a secret that he'd been obsessed with her immediately.

Imagine how insane it was to realize I could actually comprehend the way he felt about anything, let alone a mutual love interest. As our connections to Veronica grew, my disdain for him had lessened alarmingly. Orion was an arrogant prick. He could be insufferable, and sometimes I had to leave the room to keep from punching him in the face. But he wasn't a villain, nor was he my rival.

He *was* currently excelling in his role as the least interesting vampire on the planet. Orion and the Seattle clan's third in command were at an excruciating impasse. They wanted Dylan back. He refused. They wouldn't budge.

"I have no assurance that he won't be used against me at a future date. Why shouldn't I simply eliminate him here and now?" he asked pointedly. It was a solid question from a negotiation standpoint. Getting rid of Dylan would also get rid of all the problems he had dragged into the mortal realm, whether or not he meant to.

And yet, we all knew without saying that the kid would be taken back to Washington unharmed, simply because none of us wanted to force Veronica to watch him die here. That girl had found a soft spot with all of us, and she wanted to stay there—with all of us. I had no idea how in the hell it would ever work, but it was probably going to be hilarious.

"Why not, indeed?" the Seattle vamp was saying smugly. His eyes flicked over Veronica. She stood with her head down, studiously avoiding the macabre scene in the midst of playing out. Her shining wings were gone. She looked full to the brim of tired sorrow.

Orion saw it too. He glanced at Logan, then at me.

I shrugged. *Kill him, and she'll never forgive you.*

He could be kept alive, Orion mused.

Where? Logan interjected. *In the cellar? We might as well kill him.*

Yeah, and she'll never fucking forgive us, I repeated impatiently. *Don't be an asshole, Orion. Let the kid be their shitty problem now.*

Logan said, *Agreed.*

Orion gave us both reproachful stares, but he ultimately turned around and told them they could take Dylan with them as long as they got the fuck out of Alaska, and fast. He was the one who facilitated the prisoner handoff; Veronica hadn't so much as looked Dylan in the eyes since she'd brought him out. As he was being led away, though, she lifted her head once, at the same time he looked over his shoulder. Their eyes locked for a good ten seconds.

Then he was gone, lost in the considerably diminished ranks of the Seattle clan. V seemed to deflate on the spot. She didn't cry, but she sat down right where she had been standing. The decision to let her be for a while was both instant and mutual.

Instead, the three of us held court with Trent and his people. The slayers had proven to be far more resilient than I'd given them credit for—they were worse for the wear, and down a few in numbers, but by no means had they been vanquished.

"Thank you for your aid," Orion stated gravely. He paused, then offered Trent his hand. "Your generosity will not be forgotten."

Trent shook the vampire's hand. "It's not over," he said.

Orion nodded once. "I know." He gazed thoughtfully at the rapidly receding line of the Seattle clan. "What will you do now?"

Trent didn't even have to think about it. "I'm going after them to Washington," he answered. "I don't know if this is fixable, but I have to try." He was quiet for a moment. "You?"

"We'll rebuild. And when we're done, Steele

and I will have our reckoning. Whether he wants to or not." His attention turned to Veronica again, and the hard resolve in his face softened. "She will want to say goodbye to you," he remarked softly.

"She will." Trent ran a hand through his hair. "I won't be leaving right away. I figure I'll give them some time to settle in and try to make a plan. Maybe we'll get a fair fight next time."

Orion actually smiled slightly. He said, "I doubt that very much." There was no elaboration on what precisely he might have meant.

CHAPTER 33

VERONICA

Lian looked at me from across her kitchen table. "So…how are you doing?" Her face and voice were full of genuine concern, and it made me think about how I would never be as good a friend as she deserved. After all the shit I had put us through, here we were in her kitchen, talking things over—or at least I was trying to. She'd even made me lemonade.

I sighed and shrugged my shoulders. "I'm okay, I guess. It's just…" I trailed off. In the two days that had passed since the Seattle clan had taken Dylan away, I'd spent hours struggling to figure out a way to decipher my emotions. There was a storm constantly brewing inside me, and sometimes I got overwhelmed, especially when I tried to talk about it. I shook my head.

"Yeah." Lian gave me a sympathetic, sad smile. "I think that's how I'd feel too."

I didn't know how to tell her I was haunted by the image of Dylan looking back at me as he was led away with his hands still tied. In theory, I understood he hadn't been betrayed, that in fact, he had agreed to betray me first. But it was still so hard to separate that version of him from the one I loved who had lived for so long in my memories.

"V?" Lian reached over the table and took my hand. "Are you okay?"

I realized I had started to cry. Not a lot, but enough. "I thought I would only have to lose him once," I said softly.

"Oh, honey." She got up, moved over to my chair, and put her arms around me. "I'm so sorry this is happening to you."

I hugged her back the best I could, with one arm. It felt like a metaphor for our friendship as of late. "I'm sorry, too," I said. "For a lot of things."

She laughed, squeezing me tighter. "Oh, please. Yes, I was mad about it at first, and let's be real, I still don't *get* it. But look, if you're happy and they're not hurting anyone, it's none of my business. I'm glad you found something that works for you."

"You have no idea how well it works for me," I replied.

Lian grinned. "That's gross." She stood up. "Want me to call you when Trent gets home? I think he'll be leaving in the next few days. He'll probably want to talk to you first."

"Yeah." To be honest, I couldn't imagine having a conversation about Dylan at the moment. That reopened wound was still too raw, as much as I tried to conceal it. I knew better than to love him now, but the loss was still mine to grieve. "I'll see you soon."

We lingered for a few minutes longer, and then she gave me a hug goodbye, and I went out into a surprisingly sunny day. The wind blowing across the lawn smelled fresh and clean, as if the world had been renewed overnight. I stood there for a second and let it wash away all the pent-up negativity that had been festering for days. It was time to go home, where I knew my three new loves were waiting.

I gasped, arching my back at the touch of Seth's tongue between my legs. He had tied my wrists loosely to the bedposts, and I strained against the bonds, wanting more. Orion sat behind me, his lips roaming my neck and shoulder. Logan caught my mouth in a deeply passionate kiss. Orion's hands cupped my breasts, teasing each nipple.

I moaned as Logan pulled away. My head fell back against Orion's shoulder. He lifted my chin to expose the delicate skin of my throat. I felt his teeth graze there gently.

"You better not bite me," I said. "Not like that, anyway."

Seth lifted his head, much to my annoyance that he wasn't still between my legs. "Don't even think about it. We talked about that."

Orion frowned. He shifted his hips, and I felt him pressing into the small of my back. The pressure of his cock made me ache to be penetrated by any one of them.

"Is this the time?" he asked.

"No," I answered immediately. "Shut up and fuck me, please."

Seth leaned down and sucked me, hard. A jolt of wildly intense pleasure made all my muscles seize. Both my hands clenched into fists of ecstasy. Orion smiled into my skin. Leaning into him, I worked one arm free so that I could reach for Logan and pull him closer. He kissed me again, his touch tender this time. The bed creaked danger-ously under our combined weight, and then we heard a resounding crack from the frame.

Everybody paused. We looked at one another in silence until I burst out laughing.

"I told you guys we need a better bed!"

Logan ran his thumb down the edge of my jaw. "It's Seth's fault. He's very dense."

"Hey!" Seth smirked. "Let's talk when you've got your wings out. I bet they add at least forty pounds."

I looked up at Orion, whose face was a mix of annoyance and amusement. He kissed my fore-head. "What do you think?" I said. "Is this reason enough to look for a new place?"

"In Anchorage," he said. "Where we can continue to rebuild the clan."

"Listen, as long as I get my own room, I'm not complaining." I stretched to touch his lips with mine. "We'll do whatever you want."

"That's it, I'm out." Seth started to stand up.

I giggled. "No, you're not."

He sighed. "You're right. I'm not. You guys are stuck with me—including you two assholes." When he sat back down, the bed began to list to one side, threatening to slide Logan onto the floor.

Logan nodded at the dipping edge of the mattress. "See? Dense."

Orion rolled his eyes and moved both of us over to make room for Logan. He had taken some time to warm up to this group arrangement on our first attempt last night. But I had insisted for the hundredth time that he needed to learn how to share. It made me happy to see him finally starting to take that to heart.

"We will find a new house," he agreed. "At my discretion. But...I'll make sure everyone's needs are met."

"Good," I said. "Now how about my needs, right now? Because I need at least one of you to make me come."

"Anything you want, princess." Seth's tongue went back to work, Orion and Logan put their hands and mouths on my body, and I let myself be immersed in waves of bliss.

Who would have thought that three men... these monsters... these creatures of the night would help me find love again. I sure as hell didn't but for the life of me I was so glad they never gave up on me.

THANK YOU

Thanks for reading Blood Kissed.

Reviews are super important to authors as it helps other reader make better decisions on books they will read. So if you have a moment, please leave a review.

BOOKS BY MILA YOUNG

www.milayoungbooks.com

Shadowlands

Shadowlands Sector, One

Shadowlands Sector, Two

Shadowlands Sector, Three

Chosen Vampire Slayer

Night Kissed

Moon Kissed

Blood Kissed

The Alpha-Hole Duet

Real Alphas Bite

Kingdom of Wolves

Wild Moon

Wild Heart

Wild Girl

Winter's Thorn

<u>To Seduce A Fae</u>

<u>To Tame A Fae</u>

<u>To Claim A Fae</u>

Shadow Hunters Series

Boxed Set 1

Wicked Heat Series

Wicked Heat #1

Wicked Heat #2

Wicked Heat #3

Elemental Series

Taking Breath #1

Taking Breath #2

Gods and Monsters

Apollo Is Mine

Poseidon Is Mine

Ares Is Mine

Hades Is Mine

Sin Demons Co-write with Harper A. Brooks

Playing With Hellfire

Hell In A Handbasket

All Shot To Hell

To Hell And Back

When Hell Freezes Over

Hell On Earth

Haven Realm Series

Hunted (Little Red Riding Hood Retelling)

Cursed (Beauty and the Beast Retelling)

Entangled (Rapunzel Retelling)

Princess of Frost (Snow Queen)

Thief of Hearts Series Co-write with C.R. Jane

Siren Condemned

Siren Sacrificed

Siren Awakened

Broken Souls Series Co-write with C.R. Jane

School of Broken Souls

School of Broken Hearts

School of Broken Dreams

School of Broken Wings

Fallen World Series Co-write with C.R. Jane

Bound

Broken

Betrayed

Belong

Beautiful Beasts Academy Co-write with Kim Faulks

Manicures and Mayhem

Diamonds and Demons

Hexes and Hounds

Secrets and Shadows

Passions and Protectors

Ancients and Anarchy

Subscribe to Mila Young's Newsletter to receive exclusive content, latest updates, and giveaways. Join here.

ABOUT MILA YOUNG

Best-selling author, Mila Young tackles everything with the zeal and bravado of the fairytale heroes she grew up reading about. She slays monsters, real and imaginary, like there's no tomorrow. By day she rocks a keyboard as a marketing extraordinaire. At night she battles with her mighty pen-sword, creating fairytale retellings, and sexy ever after tales. In her spare time, she loves pretending she's a mighty warrior, walks on the beach with her dogs, cuddling up with her cats, and devouring every fantasy tale she can get her pinkies on.

Ready to read more and more from Mila Young?
www.subscribepage.com/milayoung

For more information...
milayoungarc@gmail.com